Leicester Writes

Short Story Prize 2019

To Alison

with love

Mary

First published 2019 by Dahlia Publishing Ltd
6 Samphire Close Hamilton
Leicester LE5 1RW
ISBN 9780995634497

Selection copyright © Dahlia Publishing 2019

Copyright of each piece lies with individual authors © 2019

The moral right of the authors has been asserted.

All rights reserved. No part of this publication may be reproduced, stored in or introduced into a retrieval system, or transmitted, in any form, or by any means (electronic, mechanical, photocopying, recording or otherwise) without the prior written permission of the publisher. Any person who does any unauthorized act in relation to this publication may be liable to criminal prosecution and civil claims for damages.

Printed and bound by Grosvenor Group

This book is sold subject to the condition that it shall not, by way of trade or otherwise, be lent, re-sold, hired out, or otherwise circulated without the publisher's prior consent in any form of binding or cover other than that in which it is published and without a similar condition including this condition being imposed on the subsequent purchaser.

A CIP catalogue record for this book is
available from The British Library

CONTENTS

Foreword ▪ *Farhana Shaikh*

The New Boy ▪ Mary Byrne	1
Our Special Words for Things ▪ Dan Brotzel	9
Because Sometimes Something Happens ▪ Debz Hobbs-Wyatt	16
Amended Endings ▪ Sharon Boyle	30
Horton Street ▪ Selma Carvalho	42
California Dreamin' ▪ Cath Barton	55
Last Dance at Plum and Woolston's ▪ Cindy George	65
The Aqua Skating Dress ▪ Emma Lee	70
Promises ▪ Thomas Morgan	81
Five Strong Colours ▪ Donna Brown	88

Asylum ▪ Patricia M. Osborne	95
Social Conditioning ▪ Dianne Bown-Wilson	99
Corundum Noir ▪ Bev Haddon	112
As Yet Unpublished ▪ Bev Haddon	120
Le Petit Oiseau ▪ Sara Hodgkinson	125
The Last of the Horse Watchers ▪ Mark Newman	133
The Edge of Love ▪ Richard Hooton	141
The Bridge ▪ Catherine Day	151
Afterimage ▪ Grace Haddon	159
Black Eyes and Love Hearts ▪ Vanessa L. Farmery	168
About the Authors	*175*
Judging Panel	*183*

Foreword
FARHANA SHAIKH

The Leicester Writes Short Story Prize was set up to celebrate the short story form and to showcase the very best new writing. Now in its third year the prize has come into its own. The quality of writing this year surpassed both mine and the judges expectations. I couldn't be more thrilled to be presenting a collection which, to me, is a masterclass on the art of writing short stories.

And the process of writing short stories is tough. Anyone who sits at the desk and attempts to write one will tell you that. What is even more challenging is writing a short story that conveys exactly what you had intended, that uses both language and form in a way that keeps your reader interested and doesn't entertain itself with too many loose threads. To be successful, short stories must be focused and have a single purpose and it is this that the writers featured in our third prize winning collection have excelled in.

That is not to say that we didn't find examples of this in stories which didn't make the longlist. The quality of writing as a whole this year was remarkable and making our selection from nearly two hundred entries down to just twenty was a challenging process.

This fills me with confidence in two things. Firstly, the love for the short story form is very much alive and kicking and secondly, there is a growing talent pool of writers who are at the cusp of a breakthrough. And co-ordinating a national prize such as this is a fascinating exercise in catching a glimpse of what new writers are writing about.

This year so many entries were inspired by #metoo, the refugee crisis, and even Brexit. There were stories which invited us into fantastical worlds and ones which allowed us to make sense of our own through sharp observation.

Our chosen longlist of twenty stories was sent off to our judging panel, chaired by Rebecca Burns and included Jonathan Taylor and Susmita Bhattacharya. As ever, I'd like to thank them for the care and attention given to all our longlisted stories, and the manner in which they conducted their deliberations.

It's always nerve-wracking to see which stories will be both shortlisted and make it to a second round of deliberation. The stories placed in our top three are all neat examples of exceptional writing.

In third place, is a writer who is no stranger to us, for she has been placed in all previous competitions. Debz Hobbs-Wyatt's 'Because Sometimes Something Happens' is so playful in form that it manages to disguise itself as a recipe. In second prize is another story that is cleverly told. Dan Brotzel's 'Our Special Words for Things' is a poignant examination of grief, love and loss told through a series of definitions.

And finally, our winning story by Mary Byrne, 'The New Boy' is a wonderful example of a story which gives voice to the voiceless and through neat observation illuminates us all.

I hope you'll enjoy the short stories chosen for this collection and that you'll return to them time and time again to reveal glorious new wonders which are so often missed on a first reading.

THE LEICESTER WRITES SHORT STORY PRIZE 2019

The New Boy
MARY BYRNE

'You're so dur-r-ty,' Miss Walsh said to the boy. 'Sit over there by the door, in front of that girl.' The teacher pointed at me. 'What's-her-name, Kathleen.'

The new boy did as he was told, sitting in the desk in front of me. He wore a black jumper over which was folded the collar of his shirt. It must have been white once but now it was dull with a brown stripe of grime. I stared at his neck: the dirt was so stuck that it had collected in patches which looked like a map. I tried to remember the atlas and any country which had the same shape.

Miss was talking to him in front of the whole class.

'What did they teach you at your last school, Liam Flaherty?'

'Dunno, Miss.'

'Are you being cheeky?'

'Naw, Miss.'

He didn't sound cheeky.

'Well, tell me. What's seven times eight?'

Everyone turned to look at him.

'Fifty-sax, Miss,' he said straightaway.

The teacher raised her eyebrows. 'What's eight times nine?'

'Seevinty-two.' Straightaway again.

'What's eleven times twelve?'

'A hunner and thirty-two.'

Someone tittered. I hate competitions and people getting at each other.

'Fifteen times,' she hesitated, 'twenty-three?'

The teacher folded her arms and smirked like she'd won. The boy paused, but only for a moment.

'Three hunner and forty-five, Miss.'

The teacher's mouth fell open.

I didn't know if he was right, but everyone cheered.

Miss thumped her desk.

'That's enough of that. Get out your exercise books.'

She threw the boy an exercise book which landed with a slap on his desk, then drew a big map of Britain on the board, her chalk squeaking, and we had to copy it in pencil.

The boy turned round to me. His eyes were dark brown and his lashes long and black.

'I havnae got a pencil,' he whispered.

I'd found the stump of one in the playground so I gave it to him.

'Put in London, Birmingham, Glasgow and Edinburgh with a dot,' the teacher shouted.

It took ages and my map was wonky so I had to write 'London' in the sea. I caught a glimpse of Liam's drawing: it was the same as the board.

'Who knows where Bristol is?' Miss asked.

There was silence – I'd never heard of Bristol – then Liam put up his hand.

'Well, Liam Flaherty, *show* me.'

She handed him the piece of chalk. Liam went out to the front. Under his ragged shorts, his bare legs were very thin. On his feet were black plimsolls although it had been raining all morning.

He thought for a minute, then put a dot near the bottom left of the map.

Miss snorted.

'Go and sit down.'

'Is he right, Miss?' someone shouted.

'Where's Aberdeen?' she asked, ignoring the question.

Liam's hand shot up immediately.

'Not you, Flaherty,' she hissed.

*

At break, after milk, everyone crowded round him. I stood at the back listening.

'How'd you get so good at everything?' Joe McBride asked. 'How're you so good at Maths?'

'Dunno. Just am.'

He wasn't tall but he seemed tall because he stood so straight and was so thin. He stared without blinking, not nasty, almost as if he was studying people like he must have studied everything else. His jumper had stains, his shorts were patched, his knees skinned, but he didn't seem embarrassed. Nobody took the mick. They were all fascinated.

'Where d'you live?' someone asked.

'Up Mill Road.'

We all knew why he was dirty. The tenements there had no bath and only one toilet on each landing.

'Why are you at this school then?'

He shrugged. 'They didnae want me at the last one.'

The bell went so we didn't get to find out why but I bet he wouldn't have told us.

For the rest of the morning, I stared at the back of his head, wondering if his brain was a different shape from the rest of us. I forgot about the dirt map. His black hair curled round. There was a freckle on the back of his left ear.

At lunchtime, I was on my own, as usual, so I looked for him. He was wandering round the edge of the playground, not joining in the boys' football games. When he passed me, I smiled but he didn't react.

'What d'you think of him then?' Yvonne Murray asked Sandra Hoyle. They both wore ironed gym slips and blouses that looked new.

'Dunno.'

'I *know* about him.'

'What do you know?'

She looked round to check no-one was listening and then leaned towards Sandra. She didn't seem bothered that I was there and I could hear.

'He got expelled from St Mary's.'

'What did he do?' I heard the excitement in Sandra's voice.

'He broke into the school?'

'What?'

'I mean after lessons when it was all locked up. He broke into Sister Scholastica's office.'

'Did he steal something?'

'Yes.'

'What?'

'An egg sandwich.'

I wanted to laugh, but then they'd notice me and make fun.

We had reading in the afternoon. Liam didn't have the book of course, so he had to move his desk and share with me. The class took it in turns to read a passage aloud. It was me and then it was Liam, last of all.

He didn't say anything, so I pointed to the beginning of his paragraph. I could hear him breathing in before he started. Was he scared? There was a long pause. The teacher was about to say something, so he began.

'Wan day, we might go t-t-to the moon. The moon is two hundred and f-f-forty thousand miles f-f-from the earth.' He paused. You could hear a pin drop. 'P-p-p people w-w-will -.'

'Stop!' shouted Miss Walsh.

My tummy went tight and I felt sick.

'Are you doing this deliberately, Liam Flaherty?'

Liam said nothing.

'He's got a stutter, Miss,' Joe McBride shouted, and everybody laughed.

'Well, if he has, at least there's something he's not good at,' said Miss Walsh, and she was smiling.

Liam had his head down so I couldn't see him.

We had writing next. The teacher didn't ask him to move his desk back.

We had to write a description of a place that we knew well, like our house. I didn't want to write anything about *my* house. What would I write? The pile of dirty washing on the kitchen floor – I tried to wash it in the bath but the sheets were too big. The dishes and things all over the place. The empty pantry but I had school dinners so I was alright. I would do a description of my granny's house instead: the funny old plates and ornaments, the lace mats, the lovely smell of polish and baking cakes. I glanced at Liam's page. He hadn't written a word. He must have known I was looking at him, for he turned towards me. I saw that he'd been crying.

I know boys aren't supposed to cry but I think that's stupid. I put my hand on his arm. He smiled at me but only with his mouth, not with his eyes.

I thought about him all the rest of the lesson. How did he learn so much? Did he really break into his school and was it just because he was hungry? Most of all, I couldn't bear that he'd cried and was hurting.

I thought of offering to go home with him, but he shot off as soon as the bell went.

'Dratted boy!' said Miss Walsh, and made us all leave a row at a time.

*

The next day was Saturday and I went to see my granny. She cut me a piece of her sponge cake and put it on a plate, one with the funny birds. We sat in her front room on the red settee with big pink cushions. She asked me how my mum was. I didn't tell her the truth, but she knew.

Afterwards, I walked through the town. It was busy with people in their best hats and coats shopping, little children trailing along behind. When I got near the library, I saw him, Liam. He wore the same jumper and shirt. He was climbing the steep steps to the revolving glass door, carrying a pile of books. Then it all made sense. He would be going there to read, and it was warm and had clean toilets. I thought about going in after him, but that was a bit like spying. I didn't have to because he came out again a few minutes later, this time carrying one very large book like an atlas or an encyclopaedia. He'd be going home now. I decided to follow him, at a distance.

He went down a side street and into a dark alley that smelt of cat's wee and rotting rubbish. There was a dog sniffing at some overturned bins. On either side were entrances to tenements. I was scared. I'd never been to this bit of town. I remembered the policeman who came to school and told all the girls to have a pencil and a comb ready in their pockets: a pencil to poke a man in the eye and a comb to scrape under his nose. I'd left my pencil at school and my comb was at home. But I needed to know so I kept following.

He went down another alley, even darker and smellier, with old tenements like ruins on either side. We reached a tenement that seemed empty. The bottom windows were all boarded up and the front steps were so crumbled away that some of them were missing altogether. Liam stopped, climbed up to the entrance, leaping over the missing steps. I waited a little, then went in after him, my heart jumping.

On the ground floor, the doors were also boarded up. Old mattresses and cookers crowded the passageway. I could hear banging doors and muffled voices above. I should have gone home, I knew that, but I wanted to see, and my mum wouldn't miss me; she never missed me. I went up the first flight, then the second, and stood on the landing. Chairs, sinks and even toilets were stacked up and covered with thick grey dust. The voices were coming from further up. I was trembling now, but I went up more flights until I reached the third floor. A door opened and light streamed onto the landing. I hid behind an upturned settee.

A man, in bare feet and wearing only a vest and trousers, came through the open door, no, *fell* through the open door, stumbling, tripping, then falling slowly, slowly until he lay in a heap. I knew immediately. The new boy came after him, tried to get him up, pulled his arm. All the man did was to bat him away as if he was an annoying fly. The boy looked up. I must have come out of my hiding place for he saw me and stared, wide-eyed. I stared back. We knew.

THE LEICESTER WRITES SHORT STORY PRIZE 2019

Our Special Words for Things
DAN BROTZEL

Anti-burst hose
Don't ask.

Bad medicine
What you called the cheap tablets I would try to get when you weren't paying attention. You always reminded me that several top manufacturers recommend Fairy Platinum, and skimping a couple of quid on some cheap imitation would actually cost us more in the long run. 'Buy cheap, buy twice,' as you always liked to say. (Not to be confused with that other bad medicine, the stuff that made you bruise like a peach and made all your muscles go numb.)

Bad fairy
A person who deliberately inflicts **bad medicine** (i.e. non-Fairy tablets) on their machine. Over time, this became your nickname for me whenever I'd done anything silly or naughty, such as overloading or giving in to my **self-storage delusion**. Or mixing up your meds or not realising that a pill organiser is an obvious **no-goer**.

Blocker
A person with a habit of stacking the machine so that the sprayer arms catch or the machine won't even shut properly.

Yep, me again. (Did you know I sometimes did a bit of blocking on purpose, just to see your comedy angry face?) (I think you knew.) (I loved that face.)

Cycle rage
Your frustration on discovering that I had mistakenly set the machine going on Eco yet again. 'It washes less intensively and takes hours,' you said. 'And we just don't have the time.'

Handling the situation
(Something you were always better at than me.) Your name for the process of going through the cutlery tray and putting all the handles the right way up or down – blades down for knives (safety first), handles first for everything else (gets all the **spoonage** off).

Intervention
The unscheduled opening of the dishwasher door mid-cycle, usually to remedy a case of **nervous ticking** or to retrieve a utensil or container that has suddenly become essential to the cook. Should only ever be done as a last resort, you always said, because untold -- though never fully explained -- damage could apparently be done to the inner workings of the mechanism by such emergency procedures. (Mind you, they saved you a couple of times.)

Kitchen cabinet syndrome
See **self-storage delusion**.

Kitchenware organisation and sanitation specialist (KOSS)
The title that you believed should be given to those rare elite beings in the world who could stack a dishwasher as well as you. 'That's a bit of mouthful,' I said. 'Just think of me as your KOSS,' you said. 'Give me a kiss, my KOSS,' I said, and you did.

Last-minute Lulu
The kind of **bad fairy** who will spend 10 minutes rearranging the whole dishwasher just to squeeze in that one extra cup that they can't be bothered to wash, even though they will almost certainly be ruining the optimum stacking arrangement in the process. Yes, OK, me again.

Mouth-to-mouth
The practice, only to be used as a last resort, of trying to blow water through the tiny apertures in the dishwasher blade, so as to remove a stubborn bit of eggshell or congealed rice. You never know when that first aid training might come in handy.

Nervous ticking
The name for that noise you made every time the machine started emitting the sort of rhythmic clicking or scraping sound that could only be the result of a schoolgirl loading error. It would take every fibre of your will to resist the urge

to stage an **intervention**. But you held on for as long as you could.

No-goer
Our term for any items that should never be put in the dishwasher, such as chopping boards, non-stick pans and bone china. You didn't like me putting my flip flops or plastic hairbrush in, even though the internet said it was OK, but I think you were just jealous because my hair wasn't falling out. But you cheered up when I found out we could put your Macmillan baseball cap in there too.

Peak plenitude
A perfectly filled, optimally full load, ready for operation. Dishwasher Nirvana.

Phillys
Name given to the mysterious person who systematically over-fills the machine because they can't be bothered to wash up a few bits by hand. I vividly remember you sighing with disappointment as you opened the door and spied another selection of only partially washed crocks: 'I see Phyllis has been in again...' The name derives, I assume, from the verb 'fill'. I'll never know for sure now.

Running on empty

A despairing phrase that describes any scenario involving the dishwasher running at less than **peak plenitude**.

Self-storage delusion
The heretical belief that the dishwasher is a mere cupboard (or **kitchen cabinet**) into which dirty stuff can be just shoved out of the way, to create a spurious impression of a spotless, decluttered kitchen. (Then again, I wouldn't have got through that week with all your family here otherwise. Had to buy a dozen extra mugs too: who knew that funerals make people drink so much tea?)

Spoonage
A disparaging term for the gunk that is left on larger utensils such as wooden spoons, whisks and fish slices when they have been lazily arranged across the lateral racks above the upper tray in such a way as to have little chance of actually getting fully clean.

Stack attack
A dishwasher crime scene where everything has just been loaded willy-nilly, with no thought given to efficient use of space or cleansing optimisation.

Stackacious!
A high term of praise for a well-stacked machine, said when a **stack-check** was found to reveal no requirement for any

remedial work. 'Wow! That was stackacious!' you sometimes used to say, of other things too. (I'm glad something still gave you a thrill, in the last days.)

Stack-check
A favourite ritual of yours where you would review my attempt to fill the machine properly before it was switched on, and correct any obvious organisational inefficiencies. Regrettably your procedures in this regard, once so robust and relentless, slacked off considerably as time wore on. 'Stack-check please!' I'd call from the kitchen; 'Stackacious!' you'd call weakly from the sofa. In the last days, you didn't even call back. But I like to think you still heard me, because once I came in and found you smiling. Your eyes were closed, but you were smiling.

Surgical procedures
Any of a range of remedial actions involving rolled-up sleeves and sump filter or circulating pump. Can rescue an apparently hopeless situation, for a time at least.

Wish-washer
A person who would kill to need to use their machine more often, now that they're only cooking for one.

Zanussi
The name I used to give to my imaginary lover. 'If you don't take your pills like a man, I'm calling Zanussi. He's waiting

to whisk me away, you know. Says he wants to sweep me up in his Whirlpool of hot love...' 'Zanussi wouldn't refuse his food like that.' It's funny, but I find I use our special names for things more than ever, now that *you*, of all people, are my imaginary lover.

Zeolite

The Siemens IQ500 machine uses zeolite in its drying process, a smart little mineral that can convert the moisture it absorbs into heat energy. This makes the machine especially good for hard-to-dry plastics and for making glassware shimmer. *Farewell, my last and best friend, purveyor of* **peak plenitude**. *Farewell, my zeolite, you who made everything shimmer.*

THE LEICESTER WRITES SHORT STORY PRIZE 2019

Because Sometimes Something Happens
DEBZ HOBBS-WYATT

- 1 tablespoon olive oil
- 25g (1oz) butter
- 1 large onion, chopped
- 125g (4½ oz) leeks, rinsed and sliced
- 280g (10oz) parsnips, peeled and chopped
- 400g (14oz) carrots, peeled and chopped
- 1 large potato, peeled and chopped
- 900ml (1 pint 12fl oz) vegetable stock
- 4-5 tablespoons semi-skimmed milk (optional)
- Salt, black pepper and freshly grated nutmeg
- 2 tablespoons chopped parsley

Monday morning. No rain. Clear sky.

Soup.

It's the kind of morning Mother used to call 'crisp'.

Crisp like leaves scuttling along Church Lane. Crisp like croutons in a bowl before they sog. Crisp like salt and vinegar.

Walkers.

Has to be Walkers.

I must add them to the shopping list.

It's the kind of morning that reminds me of Mother. The kind of morning for making winter soup.

1. Heat the oil and butter in a large saucepan. Add the onion and leeks and cook, stirring, over a medium heat, for 4-5 minutes until soft. Add the parsnips, carrots and potato and cook, stirring, for 2-3 minutes.

The house would fill up with soup.

The smells would waft up from the kitchen. They'd coat the walls of the bedroom; drift along the drafty hallways. Like a spell; a spell cast to chase away winter greyness. Before the soup, there was always greyness – like the past was a place in monochrome. A place where Mother would stand at the window; and get stuck. A place where she'd wait… for *him*, for the next time, for something to happen. It seemed as if the days folded themselves into one another. A mass of tangled bedsheets. Mother always in her dressing gown.

> Until one day something did happen.
>
> 1980.
>
> The first time Mother made winter soup.

I stand at the window, trace a crack along one of the panes; watch a line of steam rising from my tea.

> Weak, Earl Grey, milky, insipid tea.
>
> It's how I like it. How Mother liked it.

I wonder if something will happen today.

I stare at the back yard. Not as cluttered as Doreen's. Doreen over the road. Doreen who collects 'stuff'. Lots and lots of 'stuff': bin bags, boxes, carrier bags. I look at Mother's vegetable patch with its runner bean wigwams and its neatly sowed row of cabbages. It used to be the only bit of the house with any order. Not that it's much different now to when Mother was alive.

I think about carrots. Carrots, parsnips, leeks, onions, spuds.

All home grown – which is just as well; I've not left the house since 1995.

It was the same day Bet Gilroy left *Coronation Street*.

Simply Red was number one.

I found Mother hanging in the bedroom.

I lean over the gas stove and gently stir with a wooden spoon. I look at the pile of carrots on the chopping board

All I did was go out for milk. Many times I have told myself not to cry over *bought* milk.

Red top, homogenised – none of that skinny fat-free nonsense.

Mother must have had it all planned. Sent me across town to the new Tesco because the corner shop always ran out of milk by 3 pm. All the way to Tesco while she—

S-n-a-p.

I chop the last carrot, add it to the pile of veg and then scrape them off the chopping board into the pan of oil where onions and leeks sizzle.

Doreen goes to the corner shop for me now – because you can't 'home grow' everything. You can't home grow ketchup.

Or Walkers crisps.

Or angel cake.

Or Nutella.

Or newspapers.

I picture Mother, knelt down, knees pressed into the *Crompton Gazette*. She always sent me for it, never read it. I read it for her. *Anything?* No, Mother. Nothing interesting.

Good for keeping the knees dry, Giles. Yes Mother.

Good for: sowing, weeding, digging.

Sometimes she'd sing theme songs off the TV, *Cagney and Lacey* was her favourite.   Singing helps the vegetables grow she'd say.

But mostly she'd hum to them. She never did that: sing or hum or dig before 1980.

What I remember most about Mother was how she got stuck in a loop. Like the time she said there was a man in the moon and *don't you see its face right there, Giles.* Where? *There? See?* No. *There.* Where? *Oh for goodness sake, Giles. There, see it?* Yeah.

Of course I didn't see it – but I didn't want to be stuck in the same conversation.

And then in school we learned about the men who landed on the moon. I'd been five, I didn't remember it. So I said: so there *was* a man in the moon? Cue blank stare... so I added I wonder what part of the face he landed on? And she said *Face? What do you mean face?* You said there was a man in the moon and that the moon has a face. *Don't be silly, Giles.* You did. You said there was always a half we never see, like the moon has two faces. *I said that?* Yeah. *Didn't.* Did. *Giles, it's the moon, it's made of rock and it doesn't have any faces.* Yeah. It's made of rock and it doesn't have any faces.

It was another conversation I didn't want to get trapped inside.

It all changed after the soup.

Happy sounds wafted up from the kitchen. And colourful soupy smells. But before that, it seemed her life was a repeating cycle of cigarette burns and bruises.

Until *he* was gone.

I turn back from the window; glance at the calendar. Two more sleeps then I turn the page for December. Doreen loves Christmas; she'll buy more stuff: sparkly stuff and bits of tinselly twinkly stuff and she'll try to put it in my kitchen and create some 'festive cheer' she says. I let her do it, you can't argue with Doreen.

You should leave the house, Giles. Yeah, Doreen, I should.

You should start clearing the stuff, Doreen. *Yeah, Giles, I should.*

We never do – as if something centripetal stops us breaking free from ourselves.

I think about the Christmas tree under the stairs. White. Green box. A bag of red baubles. She'll be telling me to fetch it soon. *Where's your Christmas spirit, Giles?* She has to ask a few times before I eventually concede. I never told her how until *he* was gone there were no Christmas trees. No colour. And how the cupboard under the stairs had a whole other use. Or about the shouting or the *other stuff.*

And definitely no one would wrap you in tinsel and make you sing 'The Twelve Days of Christmas' and do that silly jig thing she loves. Or watch cheesy Christmas movies and fight over the purple ones in the Quality Street.

I move to the front window; peer across at number 7. Lights on. Doreen'll be up. She'll be eating eggs: soft boiled: runny – two. With white bread cut into soldiers. I look over at the row of terraces; the new moon like a thin fingernail perched on the edge of the crisp new day, before someone spoils it.

I think about my telescope, still in the shed in its box. After Father was gone I'd stare at the moon and I'd plant vegetables in sync with the lunar phases because it said you could do that in the book Mother bought me from Oxfam. 32p. The price is still there; scribbled in pencil on the inside cover.

I used to picture the water being dragged up through the soil as if the man in the moon had a giant straw. But I didn't like to think about that.

Mother had her own lunar cycles. 'Loony cycles' I told Dr Woods once. He didn't even smile. There were a lot fewer of those, or as Dr Woods preferred, 'episodes' after *he'd* gone. But they never stopped. Not completely. Not forever.

I pour stock over the carrots and the leeks; and the onions and potatoes; stand over Mother's big pot while the steam rises. It smothers my face; like a pillow. I inhale the soupy smells until I can't breathe; until I have to turn away.

When I think about it now, Mother was like the moon, part of her face always turned away, always hidden. Scarves, hoods, fingers. *Go for the paper, Giles. I don't feel well.* She must've thought I never saw what she hid, the dark side.

But that stopped when Father was gone.

We were never allowed to talk of him. Not even to Dr Woods, *especially* not to Dr Woods, who filled her prescriptions that sometimes worked and sometimes didn't when she forgot to take them, and she had to 'go away' for a bit. They assumed Father was still about and we never said.

No one has to know, Giles. No Mother. *No one has to know what we did.*

I listen to the soft simmer of finely chopped vegetables and wonder if they scream as they start to boil.

2. Pour in the stock, bring to the boil. Then simmer for 20-25 minutes until all the vegetables are tender.

I hear the waking up sounds on Church Lane: the dog at number 4 yelping to be let in and it's ages before someone does, the clink-clink that bottles make when they're dropped into the recycling, balls being slapped against concrete, and mothers shouting *Don't be late for school!* I don't remember my mother even caring if I went to school. Of course I went – but who calls a kid Giles; not someone from the east end. It always ended in tears. Bullying is not a new thing. But I could handle *them* – they were just kids.

I see the neon blur of Mr Winters' coat as he leaves number 5; he walks with big manly strides to the end of Church Lane where Doreen says a van picks him up. What kind of van? *Dunno. Why?* Just wondering. *A white one I think. Does it matter?* No. She says he works in construction, talks with an accent. What accent? *Dunno, up north.* Like a Corrie accent? *Yeah. Well no. A bit like it. More like Liverpool.* Oh.

Mother always said I was nosey. I took her place at the window when she was gone – standing, watching, wondering about people, and hoping something would happen.

Except… it already had.

The people come and go, I've seen them all: young couples who get pregnant and then get pregnant again and then they have to move to a bigger house somewhere else. Foreigners: Polish mostly, Indian, West Indian, students, druggies, old people… No one seems to stay long: just passing through. Doreen talks to them all.

She's been teaching the little Polish girl from number 10 – English – because that's what she used to be. I don't mean English, she still is English, I mean an English teacher; at Crompton Comp, before they *had to let her go* and she started to collect the stuff. Although she told me once she started collecting the stuff before that, when—

When?

She gets stuck sometimes, but not the way Mother did – mid-flow. As if the truth lies in the space that comes after the unfinished sentences.

When?

Secrets make people get stuck… and stay inside… and hoard things.

When, Doreen, love?

When George died.

That's her son. He was eight. Knocked down by a car outside her old house. 1977. The night of the Queen's silver jubilee. He was wearing a fireman's outfit, refused to change after the children's street party. She left him sleeping. Forgot to check on him. Her husband left her after that. Grief can do that. Change people. And so can guilt.

She doesn't like to talk about it just as I never like to talk about Mother. Or Father. Doreen came to Church Lane after 1980 but she was here the day Mother sent me to Tesco for red-top milk.

First time she'd spoken to me properly. Not that I remember words. She stood in the doorway after the ambulance had left... and the black van had left... and Dr Woods had left with his *I'm so sorry, Giles. I can get you the name of someone to talk to.* But I had Doreen; she was someone to talk to after they'd all left.

I remember standing in the hallway and her pulling me into her and holding me and my arms hanging limp at my sides. She smelled of sponge cake. And there we stood until she said she'd make tea and how did I like it and she said she wasn't sure what I meant by 'insipid' and did that mean lots of that red-top milk and I said yes and then I said no, on second thoughts...

She came every day after that.

Went to the funeral for me so she could tell me who turned up.

You ought to go, Giles. You might regret it. No.

No one else was there except for Doreen and Mother's older brother, William, who was the only one who stayed in touch when she started to have her episodes. And a handful of people from the church who come because the vicar asks them to. No one came back for cake or egg sandwiches or tea. No one did anything. No one knew what to do, or say because no one wants to think about how a person looks when they hang themselves and the police have to cut them down or how loud the thud is when they land on a wooden floor. No one wants to think about that.

Bodies are heavy without a soul inside them. I never told anyone that.

Of course, Mother already knew.

I prod a carrot; the blade sinks into the soft flesh. I spear a spud; to be sure before I click off the gas. The steam has coated all the windows. I wipe along the crack with the sleeve of my green cardigan, gaze out. The vegetable patch is looking so verdant.

3. Transfer to a blender or food processor and process until smooth. Return to the saucepan and pour in a little milk to thin, if needed. Season with salt, pepper and nutmeg, then stir in the parsley.

I often think that after they cut Mother down maybe she would have been a whole lot lighter.

Unburdened.

Free.

But was she?

Maybe the weight of all that guilt never really leaves.

It's not the same for me. It wasn't me who.

I was just a kid.

Sixteen.

All I did was.

Help.

To move him.

He was heavy.

It wasn't her fault.

I mean if she hadn't, he would have—

You know.

Doreen doesn't know about Father. No one does.

When people came asking we said we didn't know where he was. Only two came anyway: someone from the factory where he worked; don't remember who the other one was. Just that Mother stood at the kitchen sink drying the same spot on the soup bowl over and over while she looked out at the vegetable patch. *He left,* she said. *I don't care where he went. He left us. Good riddance.*

Doreen will be over soon for her shopping list – and for soup; she likes Mother's winter soup. She slurps. *I don't. Do. Don't.* Okay you don't. Then we laugh and she slurps louder and I think about what kind of mother she must have been to George, a fun one – caring – nice – and the kind of teacher she was – and that when you look at someone you never really know what's inside them.

 All they see are bin bags, boxes and carrier bags.

 All they see of me is a face at a window.

 No one knows anything – do they?

 Maybe one day Doreen *will* clear the stuff.

 Maybe one day I *will* leave the house.

 Maybe one day I'll get the Christmas tree out early. Surprise Doreen.

A lemon sun lifts over the Church Lane roof tops and the moon is barely a whisper now. The cabbages look ready: crisp. Like the day.

 The vegetable patch is blooming.

 I think how sometimes nothing happens. And sometimes it does.

 And when it does, some secrets are best kept buried.

 4. Reheat gently. Best not served cold.

Amended Endings
SHARON BOYLE

He says his name is Oliver and he comes with the house. Tony and I stand on the threshold of the spare bedroom which apparently isn't spare but is Oliver's and ask what this means.

'I'm a perk,' he smiles.

I recall a figure mooching in the background when we looked around the rented property. Another viewer, I'd thought vaguely. Tony remembers differently.

'The guy who owns the house – Harvey? He was chivvying Oliver to stay outside till viewing finished. I thought Oliver was just a friend or something.'

We whisper this in the master bedroom while Oliver mows the back lawn and whistles along to the radio.

'Oliver said Harvey has promised he can stay till he's found something else,' I say. 'He assured me his residence is temporary.'

'How temporary, Gail?' Tony points to his watch as if he expects Oliver to leave in a medley of minutes and seconds. 'I assumed he'd leave when we came. That would be the obvious thing to do.'

Oliver nods casually when Tony expresses his wish to live in a two-person house.

'There's a job in the pipeline,' he tells Tony.

Over the next week there is no suspicion of friends wanting to poach Oliver's time; no outside interference that surmounts his desire to stay, and no hint of a job.

'Think of me as the family pet,' he advises without embarrassment when Tony demands to know if his status has upped from wastrel to worker. 'This bungalow is massive; plenty of room for everyone.'

'Bugger that,' Tony grits out. 'You're not a pet, you're a filthy freeloader.'

To me, Oliver is more like a non-threatening, chronic illness: an overall irritant or roaming headache we can't cure. When I return home after a day of wooing reluctant employers – for I too am jobless – the house is spruced and often a home-cooked meal is on the table, but Tony and I agree the housewifery bonus does not outweigh the exasperation.

'Or his raiding of my beers,' says Tony. 'Do you know he has just two sets of clothes he likes to ring the changes with? But hey,' Tony aims his voice down the corridor, 'the lack of clothes hygiene is offset by the daily showers he has at our expense.'

Oliver disappears during week four and we glory in the absence, before discovering he is shuffling between shed and garage, ill with self-diagnosed flu and not wanting to infect us.

Tony throws up an arm. 'How magnanimous of him.'

Oliver is still poorly when he returns to the house. I offer medicine, telling him, 'When cured, you go. Tony is a photographer, an artist, which gives him license to effervescent moods. Moods I have to live with.'

Oliver squints against the kitchen light as he swallows the tablets. 'I have an interview soon.

'Really? Or is that 'really' in lie-lie land?' I fold my arms. 'By the way, we're having a housewarming party to which you're not invited.'

During the party Tony decides to 'perk-purge ourselves once and for all' and leads a drunken conga to the shed where Oliver has taken refuge with a duvet and radio. He kicks open the door, his foot splitting the wood so it sticks and has to be twisted free. As he yodels for someone to de-splinter his flesh I watch Oliver's face. It is wary and tight, but controlled. He stands within a circle of calm that deflects my slurred, shrugged apology.

Two days later Tony hobbles into the kitchen. I'm sipping wine – a calming act which helps my heart maintain a measured beat and my mind sustain a gentle burr.

'Guess what, Gail?' Tony is feverish with information. 'One of my clients knows a woman who was a previous tenant and it turns out House Intruder Extraordinaire also promised her he'd move out. He has no bloody intention of going, and why should he? He doesn't pay for rent, food or toiletries. Did I tell you he nicked my razor?'

'Yes, you said it had been returned cleaned.'

Tony dances with indignation. 'That's right. It was sparkling. The sheer effrontery. The brazen balls of the man. I am contacting Harvey.'

Tony, a non-wine sipper, likes to clash around full of shifting tempers, his being magnified by voluminous gestures. I blame his one and only photography exhibition – it turned him into a frustrated fame-chaser. His humour dial is now set squarely on 'tetchy' as he waits for the limelight to once again swing his way.

Wine-aura ruptured, I sigh and gaze at the vase in front of me. It contains a honeyed reek of back-garden flowers. A kind thought.

'How did Oliver know today's my birthday?' I ask.

Tony's eyes widen at the flowers before he plasters on a repentant face he then lies through. 'I'm out with a client tonight. Will definitely spoil you tomorrow, hun.'

Refusing to be on my own I arrange for good friend Claire to visit. We get onto the topic of the guest.

'Except he's not a guest, is he?' Claire says. 'He's been here longer than you. I wouldn't mind an odd job man around the house, especially one as gorgeous as Oliver.'

I squint. 'Odd, yes, gorgeous, no.'

'You can't see it because you're pissed off.'

'So if I cease to be pissed off, he'll magically turn into a stud?'

'He is a stud.'

'How would you know?' I laugh out two short cackles, then hiss, 'You've shagged him.'

While the rest of us carried Tony back to the house post-conga, Claire had apparently lingered and lusted in the shed.

I'm surprised I consider trust has been broken more by Oliver than Claire. Perhaps it's time to install cameras to see what he gets up to. Cadged biscuits and self-emptying tea barrels don't vex me, it's the notion of him interfering with friends or rummaging through my things, perhaps lying on my side of the bed, his head on my pillow, so that when he's sprawled in the spare room he smiles, knowing his DNA is mingling with mine and Tony's as we have sex.

'No cameras.' Tony's statement is the full-stop to that conversation when he clambers into bed later. 'I am not spending another penny on that loony-tunes house-hijacker.'

As we lie back to back my mind races along the corridor, past the kitchen and utility room and stops outside the not-spare room, wondering if Oliver is sleeping or dreaming or conniving how to slip on a wash without us yelling about it.

***

'Ollie? Great guy once you know him and I've known him since uni,' booms Harvey when he eventually answers our pleading and visits during week seven.

'What normal person lives like this?' Tony asks.

Harvey shakes his head. 'He's not normal, is he? He's a loveable but idle bugger.'

'He's a thief. He eats our food. He finished,' small pause as Tony breathes in enough air to voice the unforgivable, 'the last roll of toilet paper.'

'Look, I've had a word; he's packing and I'll swing by and collect him tomorrow.'

'He has nothing to pack but his brass neck.' Tony stands sentry at the open front door. 'Funding a third party was not mentioned in the particulars.'

'A house this size? In this area?' Harvey casts wide his arms. 'Did you not wonder about the laughably low rent? It's a sweetener.'

'Get him now.'

Harvey pauses before clutching his left arm. 'Think I feel faint.'

Tony gives a palms-up surrender gesture, rocks back on his feet and looks ceiling-ward. It gives Harvey the chance to bolt.

Tony stares after the fleeing figure, his shoulders slumping. 'I'm hitting the streets. Do some photography. See what the folks in this backside of a town have apart from faux-pas fashion. What are you doing, Gail? Still hunting down the perfecto publishing job? Accept anything; we have three mouths to feed. I'll be late home.' His kiss almost makes contact.

We used to kiss all the time: passionate, gluey kisses. When we first met he charmed me with affection – plus a flattering request to use my face to fill a wall in his exhibition. We stood in front of my celluloid features, cooing and beaming alongside his admirers. We married three months later with me assuming position on his glare-lit podium. But his ego made sure there was room for only him and when the next exhibition turned into the never-exhibition I was demoted to a 2-D wife and a one-woman audience. He doesn't realise why the hot meals and sizzling shags shrank to salads and frigidaire sex.

I head for the shower but stop short at the bathroom door. The vanity surface is talcum powdered, and the word written in the powder is Unhappy? with a sad-faced emoticon underneath.

Is it that obvious?

The author appears behind me. 'Fancy a brew?'

'With our electricity?'

Oliver crinkles out a smile. 'Promise to do all the gardening.'

'Don't you want your own place?'

'I don't believe in home ownership.'

I pause at his gall. 'Well, we do, Oliver. This house is a glitch till we get back on our dream path.'

'Dream path? Oh God, you're one of those who want to live the dream?'

I sigh. 'Well, that depends on whether I can forgive Tony's affair with a model who brainwashed him with her tits.

Oliver hesitates. 'How can you wash something that doesn't exist?'

I blurt out laughing, covering my mouth at the treachery. It's the first time I've laughed in a while.

He shrugs. 'Was that inappropriate?'

'Don't worry, I say inappropriate things too.'

'You seem very agreeable. What inappropriate things do you say?'

'Things like...let's shag.'

I've startled him. He cocks his head to the side and stares at me, like a dog unsure of its owner. He smiles, slowly. It is a beautiful smile.

After we have sex I tell him, 'There are two ways this can end. Either you leave or Tony and I do.'

'Or you stay with me and Tony goes.'

I prop up onto an elbow. 'Are you asking me out?'

'I don't believe in closed relationships. Suppose that's something Tony boy and I have in common.'

'But you do believe in nicking other folks' stuff?' I flop back onto the mattress. 'Tony says I'm not the best in bed.'

'Seems he's not the best out of it.'

This is not the confirmation I'm looking for but we have sex again before stripping the bed.

'Tony kills books,' I say, shaking a pillow from its slip. 'He bends and breaks spines, folds pages, writes in them, edits them. I used to work in publishing, in the city, before I was made redundant. Honestly, who kills books?'

'Tony the book killer?'

'He alters endings too. You know *One Flew over the Cuckoo's Nest*? In Tony's version the McMurphy guy strangles the bitch nurse and lets out all the inmates.'

'Certainly more upbeat, but unsettling to know I'm living with a guy who must have endings adhering to the Tony version.' Oliver smiles. 'He's probably cuckoo himself.'

I laugh at this, and at the fact Tony's not the only cuckoo in the house.

I do not laugh when Tony tramps in after work wanting his dinner straight away because he's 'been trawling Shitsville in an attempt to photograph someone who's above pond-life.'

'I've been trawling too,' I huff, 'through the recruitment pages. Low-waged, part-time jobs are all the rage.'

'You've had time to trawl and cook.' He stops, frowns and sniffs. 'What's that smell?'

'What?'

He steps closer. 'That's the smell of...'

'What?'

He glares at me. 'Sex.'

***

I escape from his phlegm-filled fume to buy some wine. By the time I return he's filled a rucksack with my things and slung it in the hall.

'I'm leaving?' I ask.

'You are.'

'But I've ignored your indiscretion.'

A missed beat before, 'Pardon?'

'You were with her on my birthday, weren't you?'

Another pause. 'She means nothing.'

'You're a weasily shit, Tony.'

We both turn to see Oliver lurking in the shadows.

'Such a shit,' Oliver repeats. 'A pompous, oily shit. Gail's worth ten of you.'

Silence balloons as Tony collects himself to register that yes, the freeloader has enough brass to his neck to interfere and insult. He hyena-hunches his shoulders while Oliver blanches but stands his ground. Tony takes this as an affront, grabs Oliver's arms and flings him against the wall so forcefully the plasterboard dents.

'Tony,' I shout. 'Calm down.'

Tony is beyond calming down and lunges at Oliver like a goaded bull. I mentally will on Oliver but he goes down again, taking the phone table with him.

'Still up for a thrashing?' Tony jeers, drawing back a foot to aim at Oliver's head. But then he stops. His knees crumple. His waist folds over. His head thuds against the carpet. I stand above him holding the phone.

He is slow to forgive, emptying his mouth of insults until I explain that a knockout is preferable to prison and don't worry, I'll go see if our guest is all right.

I catch Oliver skulking at the front door working up the nerve to cross the threshold. The controlled look has gone.

'I should leave,' he whispers.

'Wait there.'

I head to the bedroom where Tony is sitting on the bed pretending to read a book, refusing to face Oliver and wondering if he has gone too far.

'You were going to kill him, Tony. There's no need to wonder.'

'What are you doing?'

'Giving him your clothes since you wrecked his.'

'That's Saville Row. Give him the M&S stuff.'

'I am giving him your expensive togs and you'll shut up about it. Think yourself lucky he's not pressing charges.' I fill a holdall, walk out and hand it to Oliver.

'You need to leave too,' he says.

I see from his earnest expression that he wants me to hook his elbow and trot down the path with him.

I point to the rucksack. 'I may do, see, Tony's handily packed for me.'

Oliver brightens until I ask, 'Where will you go?'

He clears his throat. 'No idea. I've been here for eight years. I've grown used to being...' he splays his hands.

'A perk?' I suggest.

I watch him walk away. He'll probably go to Harvey's and potter around till even Harvey's patience dries out. When he's out of view I slip on my coat and shoes, lift the rucksack and make to leave. But I stop.

What do I look like, standing on the door ledge, feet pointing to the outside world? As deflated as a week-old balloon, that's what, through years of being agreeable. I close the door and stride into the bedroom.

'I am editing me out of our marriage, Tony. From now on it will be the Gail-only version.'

Tony hands me the book he's been reading. 'Take a look.'

It's *Gone with the Wind*. I scan the open pages. 'You've highlighted something. 'As God is my witness I'll never be,' ah, you've scored out 'hungry again' and replaced it with 'unfaithful again'. My, what editing.' I look up. 'You leave tomorrow.'

'What? You're serious? Tomorrow?'

'Tomorrow is a new day where we don't have to act like funfair high-strikers hammering at ourselves all the time. It's not me, it's not you, it's us.'

Tony slides off the bed, hitches up an Elvis sneer and picks up his camera from the side-table. 'But mostly you.'

'Out.'

I listen to him pace along the corridor, to the room that tonight is not empty, not spare – it's his.

Horton Street
SELMA CARVALHO

The small house down the street is festooned with balloons. It's hot under the June sun. Hottest summer in London since records began. There's a drought warning on the second-hand car radio.

Bone dry birch bark

Water me a droplet

Ripen me a couplet

Then these white balloons sucked full of air appear on the no. 19 door. They look like gelatinous jelly fish beached on a red-sanded shore. They swing slightly during the day and squeak eerily at night. But they stay on the door. Everyone is talking about them. Anne Gilbert went around to the house and now all of Horton Street knows why the balloons are there. The Prime Minister is coming to visit no. 19, and this story could be called The Prime Minister Comes Around.

Really? We ask with curiosity and shock.

'But why?'

No one knows the answer to that question.

Maggie and Len are as ordinary as the rest of us. Granted they have eleven children while we have two or three. Maggie is only in her twenties, brown-haired and small, but she looks worn as the day. And Len always has paint on the blue overalls he wears when he comes to pick up the kids.

The primary school is at the mouth of Horton Street. From there the road flows upwards, where summer flowers blow petals over boundary walls and serrated rows of red roofs line upright until they curve and meet Rawley's Place. From these houses emerge mums every morning with snotty-nosed kids cleaving to their hips, and others, fair-faced and fleet-footed, running ahead of them much too fast to contain. But the mums, they let them run, because it is a quiet street and if a car does come by it will have the good sense to brake in time. We, Asian mums, natter on about 'mine one' as if other people are lining up to claim custody of our tots. All the mums stop for a while outside of Big Thomas's house. Thomas sits there, early morning, selling packets of sweets, hoping to catch the eye of those little ones off to school.

'Everything is 50p,' Thomas says, directing the children's greedy, bug-eyes to the sweets. Sometimes their tiny, grasping fingers reach out to touch those sugar-flecked packets, and Thomas lets them.

Solid man Thomas. Like an oak tree with lumber-jack limbs. He can easily break a neck with those hands. When he isn't selling sweets, he sits there anyway, saying good-mornin' to the children that pass by. I don't think he ever makes money off what he's selling because let's face it, it's just rubbish in sealed plastic. The mums toy with it but never buy anything. I think Thomas sits outside his house because he's afraid of what's inside, and he likes having little children gather about him in the morning.

The only time Thomas is not outside is when a police car's parked up. It's not unusual to see a police car parked at one or the other house, because there's been a 'disturbance' in the night, or to find vomit on the pavement, beer bottles caught in hawthorn hedges, leaky condoms capped on gates or garbage fly-tipped in corners. None of that is unusual. You just walk past it, don't you? You look the other way and try to focus on the flowering ferns, the dogs doing their business or cats climbing out of windows. You smile to yourself and think, one day I'm going to escape all this. Hope is that translucent thing that claws its way into the human ribcage and settles there. We can inherit hope from other ribcages especially if our bones have not yet hardened against the world. One of the school teachers got a job in Richmond and the school had such a do for him. Richmond, imagine that.

Richmond dreams of gardens deep

Lion-guarded gates swallow my sleep.

So, we have no idea why the Prime Minister is coming around to No. 19. And we don't feel right to ask. Why would we? We keep behind our lace-curtain windows. We know what we know and no more than that. Our weary eyes stand watch over the cruel asphalt river cleaving right through us, separating us like a clothes line: whites on one side, coloured on the other.

*

The next week the balloons are still up.

Jaya calls me and asks, 'Should we do something for the Prime Minister's arrival?'

'What do you mean? Like meet her at the station?'

'Don't be a smart-ass. She's not going to come by train, innit?'

'Well she might. Just to prove she's in touch with the common people.'

'Stop that. Nobody likes a smart-ass. Why don't you say positive things for God's sake?'

'What do you want to do?'

'We could organise a street party.'

'Would that be the browns or the whites organising it?'

Jaya is annoyed as she often is with me. Jaya has the laudable ability to blend in, to laugh loudly, to cosy up to teachers and volunteer her time at school. I watch the six o'clock news - alone. Yet, who can decipher the codes of friendship? They are held together with thin welts of need, opportunity and proximity. Jaya and I are different in ways we don't acknowledge. For if the heart calibrated for every variation and imbalance, the fortunes of friendship would run dry.

'You know Gina Salter?'

'The receptionist at the school? Ginny?'

'Yes. She took me aside and asked if we should do something?'

'She's never so much as looked at me. You remember the Year 4 museum trip?'

'Yeah.'

'I went to Reception to sign mine one up for that. Gina-Ginny pushed the register in my face and left. I was in tears. I am not invisible, you know?'

'Still,' Jaya ignores my distress and carries on undeterred, 'this is an opportunity for all of us to come together.'

I snort my disapproval. It is not going to work. Lurking beneath the quiet of Horton Street are fissures deep; the disappearing parks and budget-shredded libraries, the run-down school and the over-stretched local surgery, the floundering community centre and crowded communal pool pulsate with anger and other sharp-edged objects which challenge people to give of themselves when they have naught to give.

*

The day we are supposed to meet Gina to discuss the street party, Billy White disappears from school, and this story could easily be called Billy White Disappears.

We stand trembling at the school gate where we've come to pick up our kids. We are all worried; the last he'd been seen was at P.E, and then while the other kids had returned to class, Billy White had simply disappeared. Horton Street is quiet but at least two nationally known child molesters have been arrested in the borough and no one wants Billy White to end up that way. We all know Billy is slow. Without saying as much, Billy belongs to all of us, and we look out for him.

Billy is the eldest son and his mum is reed thin whose ungrateful body has ripened four times to bless her with children. And she never has money on her because you can hear her in the morning, off her coke-head, mouthing obscenities at someone or other she owes money to; prodding Billy along like a mule, his red hair all aflame. We hear 'poor Billy' muttered here and there, as poor Billy bears the brunt of his mother's temper.

Pigeon's peck at Billy's brain

Blood-red runs an old stain

Jaya and I link arms and feel the vibrations of loss parents feel when a child obscures from their line of vision. We wait at the school for news of Billy. Grey clouds bruise the sky and a chill wind sweeps over the grassy mounds of open ground. Jaya's daughter and my two sons are at the swings. Finally, we motion to them to come to the gate where we are stood.

'It must be the Arabs at the end of the street that took him,' Jaya says.

'Why would they? They have enough of their own.'

'They don't mix with us, innit? They keep to themselves.'

'We don't mix with them either.'

'The street party would have been a good idea,' Jaya says bleakly.

Horton Street has grown. It is peopled with new faces freshly arrived from war-torn parts of the world. In their eyes, we see violence and a threat to our quiet street. We imagine them with bombs in their rucksacks and knives tucked in their pockets. But we see them ruffling their children's hair and kissing their cheeks. Then it matters less which God they pray to or what language they speak. Children make you listen to the murmurations of the soul and they bond you with fellow parents in a universal incantation of prayer.

'It's going to rain,' I say, squeezing her hand, 'and we're going to have your street party.'

We walk the short distance home in silence.

That evening I pace my ugly-tiled kitchen. I put white bread in the toaster, watch it pop, butter it in scoops before tossing it in the bin. I clack plates and clink glasses, and stack them on the dish rack. My cat stares at me in silence curled up on a shelf high above. Upstairs my sons are asleep, and the house fills with the hush of their breathing. I wait by the phone. Ring, please ring. Drops of rain streak my window. I think of the balloons at no. 19 and how they will not survive the night.

It is about eight when the phone jumps me out of my skin. It's Jaya. Her breathing is ragged. She is struggling to get the words out.

'They found him,' she says at last.

'Is he alright?'

'Yes.'

My sigh of relief echoes to mothers - swirling in dark hollows - waiting by the phone to hear news of their children.

'Where was he?'

'It turns out, Billy walked right through the school gates?'
'Just like that? Was it his dad who took him?'
'No. Billy walked past the school gate and kept on walking. He walked down the road and made it all the way to the train station.'

My heart skips a beat. Billy could have fallen down the tracks. He could have been nabbed by human traffickers and sold to a free-range egg farm. He could have been molested by a man in a large overcoat.

'Then he went to Salim-Bhai's shop and asked for a coke.'
'And?'
'Salim-Bhai asked him where his mother was, and he just stood there.'
'Did Salim-Bhai call the police?'
'He did one better. He handed him a coke, a sandwich, some biscuits, and then marched him back to his house where the Head Teacher, Billy's mam and the police were waiting.'

*

Gina, Jaya and I meet at the Horton Tandoori Palace. It smells of clarified butter and grilled chicken. That's the only restaurant left on Horton Street. The Horton Fish & Chips is now a Domino's Pizza.

The waiters spring like rabbits as we enter. Gina's strapless dress curves over her sloping breasts and a bump I haven't noticed before. Our gummy table has been wiped with a dishcloth. Gina sits across from us complaining about NHS appointments for her bump. I give her a sympathetic look. I let her know straight away that I voted for Brexit. Even though, I'd said to Jaya at the time, that the UKIP posters popping up in some neighbourhood windows were making me uncomfortable. Gina smiles, pushes back a bottle-dyed curl, and says she voted Remain. An awkward silence descends on our table. I motion to where the waiters are a starling swarm. A bearded man materialises at our table with three laminated menus. The menus are so big, we disappear behind them.

'I'll have a glass of Shar-don-ney,' I say.

'Madam, we serve alcohol only after 7 O'clock,' he informs me, pulling out a notepad and pencil. His arms are strong, his fingers thick.

'What time is it now?' I ask.

'It's 6:30.'

'Can't you make an exception?'

The waiter turns down his pencil, licks his lips, and waits for me to change my mind. I notice gravy spills on his serving apron. The spills repulse me. I hate the way his fingers stroke the pencil, the way his lips move when he says 'madam'. I hate his curling lashes, his lilting voice, his beautiful, bearded face. His body is rock hard, his limbs are long.

Let me read you all the love stories of the world

Taste of my deceitful mouth a desire so achingly old

We settle on three cokes and a plate of Punjabi samosas.

Gina empties the plastic bag she is carrying onto the table. White sheets of paper leap out. She flattens them with a thick palm and says, 'These are the names and telephone numbers of families living on Horton Street. There are about fifty families.' Her teeth are yellow and large when she speaks, like a steel trap opening and closing. Jaya and I lean forward to get a closer look. The table squashes our breasts. The small Arial font strains our eyes. We notice that Gina has segregated the names into two columns, marked 'English' and 'Asian'. The waiter arrives with our order. He licks his lips and places our food and drinks on the table. Then he retreats to a corner. The coke fizz nuzzles our noses.

'Who is going to call these people?' Jaya asks.

'I'll ring the English families and you two can ring the Asian homes,' Gina says, taking a large bite of her samosa and wiping her oily hands on a paper napkin.

Jaya nods her agreement. She's relieved.

I look into Gina's face and find her smiling eyes. They are blue as a summer sky. Gina pierces right through the Brexit-voting-Chardonnay-Me. She smells that rancid second-generation Southall ambition in me. She knows my house is cluttered with Maths and English preparatory books for the boys; stacked high with brochures on Hounslow tuition centres and Slough grammar schools. She knows of that old pair of sneakers I wear to go jogging past Indian sweet shops; she knows my skin longs for sequined silks and that my house smells of cardamom and turmeric. She knows I want to fuck that beautiful, bearded waiter. Sitting here in a third-rate tandoori restaurant, she knows I am brown in ways which even I can't fully comprehend, and that my emotional cartographies defy boundaries, seeking sheltering shores far away from Horton Street. Gina Salter knows I am a half-formed person, but she is wise enough to know that she is too.

*

I don't see Gina at the school the next day. Jaya calls up and says, 'Are you alone?'

'Alone as in lonely or alone as in by myself?'

'Don't be a smart-ass.'

'Yes, I'm alone.'

'Can you come out?'

'It's ten in the night.'

'Meet me at the Green.'

'Alright. I'll be there in five minutes.'

The sky is lit by a June sun, but the streets are still. The Green is empty of children at this time. Someone has left a bicycle parked on a tiny hill and a deflated football lies amidst a boundary of strewn chip packets and sweet wrappers. Jaya hurries down the street. She waves when she sees me. I can tell something is not right.

'What is it?' I ask.

'It's Gina. There's been a disturbance.'

'What happened? Was she burgled?'

'No. It's her husband. She's had to call the police. They're charging him with rape.'

'What? Who did he rape?'

'Gina.' This story could be called Gina Gets Raped.

'I don't believe it. I saw them a week ago at Tesco's. They seemed happy.'

Jaya and I are silent, not knowing what to make of it all.

Who can decipher the codes of coupling? Who can hear the soundless violence of intimacy? The subtle pressure on the wrist, the bruising on the arm, the savagery of silence, the recurring leitmotif of melancholy. All these are contained within the walls of virtuous lives and edifices of normalcy. Who will tell your stories when you've been in the wars?

'It would have been worse,' Jaya says, 'but Big Thomas heard 'em, innit? Thomas went in and clocked him one.'

'What will happen to the street party now?' I ask.

'I'm going to call all the families – white, brown – I don't care, I'm going to call them one by one,' Jaya tells me.

I understand why the street party is important to Jaya.

Take me to Richmond, Horton Street

Lay me down at her gilded feet

O winged angel seraphim

Bring me home in a dream

The sky is beginning to darken. A hesitant moon makes its way into the fading blue. I look at what I think are the frayed edges of the street. But the edges are not frayed. They are unfurling to make more stories part of our lives; for what do streets remember? They remember the children who imperilled themselves and those who rescued them; the lonely who sat on pavements and the strangers who comforted them; the young who kissed in the shadows and the bruised who sheltered under lamps. They remember the houses from where emerged nurses and poets, teachers and travelling circus acts who healed us. They remember the new people who came looking for a better life and the old neighbours who made room for them. That summer, Horton Street would remember the bunting and the food laid on tables borrowed from the Tandoori Palace, lined end-to-end until they snaked out of sight and into Rawley's Place. And it would remember the rejoicing and the oneness that rained on our heads that day.

California Dreamin'
CATH BARTON

After days and days of sunshine, just like the summers when she was young, it's raining again. Mairwen peers out of the smeared window at the smeared sheep on the Welsh hillside and sighs. The slugs will be out heading for her young plants. If only Pedr was here…

A sharp rap on the door makes her jump. She isn't expecting anyone. The postman hands her a stiff buff envelope and runs back to his van, head down. Mairwen stands there in the doorway, gazing at the rain, the envelope and back at the rain. The postman drives off with a skid of wheels in a stony puddle by the gate. Something else she would have asked Pedr to see to…

Mairwen has forgotten that Pedr used to get under her feet in the small kitchen. She puts the envelope on the kitchen table and goes to see where the dripping noise is coming from. She finds the leak up in the bathroom. And sighs again. She puts on her wellies and raincoat and heads down the lane to her next door neighbour's house. There's no answer to her knock and Mairwen stands in the porch watching the rain. Trying to think what to do next. If Pedr had been here…

She heads home. There's an unopened envelope on the kitchen table. Mr Sniff the cat lifts his paw, the way he does when he wants attention. Did she give him his breakfast?

She pours some biscuits into his dish, just in case. Mairwen takes the kettle to the tap, fills it and makes coffee for herself and Pedr, one spoonful for her, one and a half for him, he likes it strong. It's Saturday, Pedr always liked a lie-in on Saturdays. She sits at the kitchen table, picks up the envelope. The stamps are foreign, American by the looks of them. Who on earth can it be from? She gets a knife, slits the end of the envelope and pulls out the papers inside.

There's a postcard from her Pedr, it's definitely his writing. The picture seems to be of some kind of monster. Mairwen puts the postcard on the table. She needs her reading glasses, which she knows she had by the bed last night. At the top of the stairs she hears the dripping again and goes looking to see where it's coming from. There's a puddle on the floor in the bathroom. She goes downstairs to get a bucket. Up and down again and she's back at the kitchen table, able to drink her coffee at last, though it's cold now. Why has she made two cups? And she still hasn't got her reading glasses.

Mairwen finds her glasses on the kitchen dresser. Now she can see that the picture on the postcard is of an owl sitting in a tree. Pedr's got a thing about owls, has had ever since that incident in the museum. She never quite understood what happened but it was after that that he applied to the film school in America.

She flicks over the postcard.

'The time has come Mam!!!' she reads. *'Here are your tickets. No more talking about it Mam – You Are Coming!!! Mr Jones will drive*

you to the airport. All you have to do is pack your bag. Bring sunglasses! And a nice frock for the show!! Love from Pedr.'

Mairwen reads it twice. Pedr has sent her plane tickets. To go to Los Angeles. The place where he lives now and makes films. She looks at the date on the ticket, then marks it on the calendar on the kitchen wall. She uses the big marker pen hanging there. Then she picks up the phone. There are three buttons on it – 1 for Pedr, 2 for Mr Jones and 3 for someone else she can't quite remember. She presses number 1. After about ten rings there's a muffled answer,

'Who is this, it's the middle of the damned night…'

Mairwen hangs up, confused. Pedr had told her to ring any time. After a few minutes the phone trills. She leaves it for three rings, then picks it up and lifts it slowly to her ear.

'Hello,' she says in a small voice.

'Mam, I've told you before about the time difference… but anyway never mind, you got the tickets then?'

'I did, son, I did.' Mairwen doesn't want to say the wrong thing, so she doesn't say anything else.

'So, you okay Mam? Mam?'

'I'm okay, son.' She doesn't really feel okay, but she doesn't want to worry Pedr.

'Mr Jones will get you to the airport, make sure you're in plenty time for the plane. Don't worry about a thing, Mam. See you soon! Got to go now, need my beauty sleep.'

Mairwen hears a giggle and then a click as a receiver is put down several thousand miles away. Another sharp rap on the door makes her jump.

'Only me,' says a voice, as a stooped man opens the door and walks in with a dog, which shakes itself violently, causing the cat to flee and Mairwen to sigh.

'Oh, Ifor!'

'Only a drop of rain,' he says. 'It'll soon dry, Mair. See you got the tickets from your boy then,' he says, nodding at the papers on the table.

Mairwen sinks onto a chair and bursts into tears. The man, who is her neighbour, Ifor Jones, swallows, sits down next to her, quietly, and puts a hand on her forearm. They sit there together for some time, the dog panting at their feet and the rain noisy on the window pane.

'I'm sorry, Ifor,' she says in the end.

'No need for any sorries, Mair, no need at all,' he says. 'The boy's a long way away, you're bound to miss him.' He waits, but Mairwen doesn't reply.

'Any chance of a cup of coffee?' he says.

'Of course,' she says, wiping her arm across her eyes and scurrying up to the tap with the kettle again. 'And I must have a biscuit somewhere.'

They sit and drink coffee together and Ifor says he can hear a drip, so he goes to look.

'I'll get up a ladder when the rain stops,' he says. 'Probably just leaves in your gutter. Keep the bucket there for now.'

Mairwen can't think what bucket he's talking about, but later she sees it in the bathroom and realises, in a moment of clarity, that Ifor must have put it there.

Three weeks later, Ifor drives Mairwen to the airport. It's an early May day.

'So many lovely greens, Mair,' he says. 'I wonder what the countryside will look like in California.'

Mairwen smiles at him. 'California?' she says.

'Yes, where Pedr lives. You know.' And he starts singing a tune he knows she knows, and she joins in.

Mairwen knows all the words of the song, it's California Dreamin' from the 1960s when she was young, and as she sings her face lightens.

'If you feel worried on the way, that's what you need to do, Mair, sing that song.'

Which she does, though when the person sitting next to her on the plane turns and frowns she stops singing out loud and just does it in her head.

As the plane comes in to land Mairwen takes her first look at Los Angeles. Houses stretching for miles, and everyone seems to have a swimming pool. Pedr hadn't said anything about bringing a swimming costume. It worries her that she hasn't got one, so she starts singing the song again in her mind. She's still doing it as she walks off the plane and into the terminal. Then, suddenly, she's through and there's a big crowd of people holding up placards with names and there's hers – MRS MAIRWEN DAVIES – and she looks round in case there's another woman with the same name, but no, it's really for her, and as she approaches him the man holding the placard is smiling and calling out now in a very loud voice.

'Hey!' he says. 'Welcome to LA Mrs Mairwen Davies!'

It's not Pedr. Mairwen was expecting Pedr. This is a small man. A small brown man with an accent that is different from the American ones she's heard on television.

'I was expecting my son,' she says to the man.

'Sure lady,' he says. 'My name is Henriques. Mr Peter asked me to come along for him. He has business today. He says to tell you he'll see you for dinner around eight. In your hotel. No worries lady, it has a very nice pool, your hotel. You can relax. Take a cocktail while you're waiting. Now please, follow me.'

And without waiting for her to reply he takes hold of her luggage trolley, wheels round and sets off. Mairwen has to nearly run to keep up with him. And her mind is a-flutter with worries – why had Pedr not come, who was this man and where was she going to find a swimming costume? She sets the song going in her mind, but it gets jostled by all the worries and she can't get the tune right.

In the car Henriques chatters away about the places they are passing, pointing out the Hollywood sign on the hill and the gates to various places where famous people she has never heard of apparently live. Fortunately he doesn't seem to need his passenger to respond. Mairwen is tired after the flight, and the smooth motion of the car and the sing-song tones of her driver soon send her into a fitful sleep, during which she has vivid dreams about crawling monsters; as soon as she is alone in her hotel room she has to check under the bed and behind the curtains, in case. Relieved at finding nothing, she takes off her shoes and flops onto the enormous bed, where this time her sleep is undisturbed by bad dreams.

She is woken by the phone ringing. It's still light, but she has no idea of the time.

'Hey, Mam, croeso iawn!! I'm coming over. Be with you in twenty!'

Pedr rings off before Mairwen is fully awake. She splashes her face, changes into her second-best frock and is exploring the balcony of her room when there's a knock at the door. It's been two years. Pedr, who was a big lad when he left, is now even bigger. Mairwen can barely get her arms around him.

'Mam, Mam, we gotta go eat, I'm starving. You fancy hickory burger or quesadillas?' Pedr is bouncing on his toes in his excitement.

Mairwen holds up her hands. 'Slow down!' she says.

But, for all that she has no clue what a hickory burger is, or quesadillas, she can't help laughing, so relieved and delighted is she to see her boy.

'Chips and egg?' she asks. 'Does your big city do that?'

'Sure thing, Mam, but you has to call them French fries,' he says. 'You ask for chips and they'll give you crisps.'

Later that night, lying in the big bed with lights from the traffic on the freeway outside playing on the ceiling, Mairwen finds herself thinking she would like to ring Ifor Jones back home in Wales and tell him about this place where not just her son, but the hotels, the beds, the drinks and the food are all super-sized. But she isn't sure what time it would be in Wales, and Ifor's number is somewhere but she doesn't know where and, next thing, sleep has claimed her once more.

Ifor, though, is well aware of the time differences and the following day, when he has worked out it will be 9am in Southern California, he rings the hotel.

'Hello Mair,' says the familiar Welsh voice when she picks up the receiver. Mairwen can't remember what she ate the night before, but Ifor is used to that. She knows who he is, that's the main thing. And she says that yes, Pedr's looking after her just fine.

Today Pedr takes his mother to the beach. They sit in a bar and he orders coffee and she doesn't say she'd rather have tea, because he looks happy, does her Pedr, and Mairwen doesn't want to spoil that. She asks him about the film and he says it's difficult to explain.

'Best wait and see, Mam,' he says. 'Tomorrow, it is. You relax in the day. Swim in the hotel pool, why don't you? I'll come for you at 9pm.'

Mairwen has a sinking feeling when he mentions swimming, but she can't think why.

'You've brought your costume, haven't you?'

She remembers she has no swimming costume and shakes her head.

Pedr just laughs and says she can buy one, but when he's gone and she looks in the shops in the Mall by the hotel she's horrified at the prices.

But in the morning Mairwen has a rush of blood to the head. She buys a costume, she goes swimming and, daringly, she orders a tuna burger with crushed avocado and wasabi tartar for her lunch. After that she sleeps. At 8pm she gets a call from the hotel reception, reminding her that her son will be picking her up in an hour. She's surprised, wondering why he would come so late.

'It's for the film showing, M'am,' says the girl on reception, who has been told by Pedr about his mother's forgetfulness.

'Ah!' Mairwen knew there must be some reason why she had bought her best frock.

The film is a 3D animation, featuring owl-like monsters and a lot of blood. Mairwen takes off the special glasses and closes her eyes after the first five minutes, but the sound is too loud for her to go to sleep. She tries to sing California Dreamin' in her head, but the sounds get muddled up and by the end of the film she has a headache. She doesn't tell Pedr this though, when he takes her through to a room where there are lots of men, all big like him. They're all laughing and talking really loudly and she can't understand a word anyone is saying so she just smiles.

'Fab evening, eh, Mam?' he says when he takes her back to the hotel.

She's too tired to speak now so she just nods.

'Yeah, you're tired. I know. All the excitement. You get used to it when you live here. Sweet dreams, Mam. It was super-great to see you.'

Afterwards Mairwen doesn't remember whether she had sweet or bad dreams that night. She doesn't see Pedr again – he sends Henriques to drive her back to the airport the following day. And when she gets back to London and Ifor Jones meets her off the plane she's very quiet for the whole of the long journey up to North Wales and home.

Next day Ifor calls round and finds Mairwen crying at her kitchen table. He sits down beside her and puts his hand on her arm. His dog stays quietly at their feet. The evening sun is striking on the back of the cat stretched out on the window sill.

'It's lovely to have you home, Mair. Let's sing now,' he says. And he takes told of her hand as they sing California Dreamin' together, quite softly, and outside an owl hoots, as if it's joining in the song.

THE LEICESTER WRITES SHORT STORY PRIZE 2019

Last Dance at Plum and Woolston's
CINDY GEORGE

Everyone in this factory's an idiot except for me and Kimberley. They haven't got a clue about anything except for making crisps. We're the only ones who even watch Top of the Pops. Kimberley's alright, she comes down Topper's with me on a Friday for a dance and a laugh. I've got frosted eyeshadow and I can dance in platforms, so they never guess I'm not eighteen.

The other women here are all old, so they never think anything's funny unless it's Brian showing us his birthmark again. They all wear headscarves like the Queen, except brown at the front from the cigarette smoke. The men are brown all over, with their brown socks and their brown suits. I bet they've even got brown y-fronts under, but I haven't said that to Kimberley. She'll say I've been thinking about it. I've never seen a woman in a suit, only that lady who sometimes reads the news on the telly. If I ever had a suit, it wouldn't be brown. It'd be a purple and silver one, with flares and a big kipper tie.

It's all women on the production line, we do the cleaning and the cutting and the frying and the bagging. I always smell a bit like cheese and onion till I wash my hair on a Saturday. Sometimes the men come to stand and watch us work. Then they're off, back up the management staircase, the big posh one that smells of polish. That one's only for them and their brown shoes. When I go to the offices to get told off, I have to use the back stairs. The only time a woman can go on the management staircase is if she's cleaning it.

'Unless we get a female manager,' says Mr Woolston, and everyone laughs, because he tells us to.

I get half an hour for my dinner at twelve o'clock. Normally I nip home for some bread and jam. In the afternoon, we're allowed to eat the crisps that have gone wrong, out of a big plastic bucket, all mixed together. The clock's going slower than normal today, though. What if it's wrong? It'll spoil everything.

Five to. I'll sing two songs in my head, then it'll be twelve. I hope Kimberley remembers.

I went to Careers Advice at school once, they said I might be clever enough to get O levels, and maybe be a secretary or a teacher one day. I don't fancy teaching, I've got a little sister. Kids don't know anything, and they shout all the time, and they're always sticky, and they smell of sicked-up rice pudding. And I can't be a secretary, I don't like wearing blouses. I'd rather be at the factory with all the old women and their sensible cardigans. The men in suits never wear cardigans, and I don't either. I might get cold, but at least I don't look thirty.

It's not as if I like working at the factory, but it's nice to have money of my own. I've been saving up for a bomber jacket. I bought some silver nail polish with my first pay, but when I still had it on at work on Monday, the supervisor saw and tried to make me scrub it off with bleach. I knew that wouldn't work so I scraped it off with my teeth instead. The polish set solid in the bottle after a couple of weeks of not using it, but I still keep it on my dressing table to look at. I wish I could have worn it today.

Twelve o'clock! I'm not meant to run, but I do.

Kimberley's by the toilets, bright red and holding her brother's little plastic transistor radio. We don't say anything, just hold hands and keep running.

Halfway up the management staircase, there's a little landing, a bit like the mini stage at Topper's, where they sometimes have a girl dancing in her bathers. We put the radio on the step and turn it all the way up. It's not very loud, but it's a good song. Anyway, that's not even the point. We just dance. We copy all the actions we've seen them do on telly, even the ones that look a bit rude. We are pop stars.

Half the factory's at the bottom of the stairs now, not daring to set foot on the steps to get us. We pretend they're our audience, and wave at them.

The song's nearly finished by the time Mr Woolston drags us down the staircase, then back up by the back stairs to his office.

*

Kimberley kept her job, but I had to go and work in Fine Fare. We never fell out, but a few weeks after, we were at Toppers and we saw the lad from the butcher's - the one we called Fluffy, because he reminded us of Kimberley's mum's cat. He asked her to do the Bump with him. Kimberley didn't come out as much after that.

I was a bridesmaid, even though I wouldn't wear the coral chiffon maxi dress she picked out for me. And of course we stayed in touch. Mates are mates. But never so much as when you're seventeen.

They moved into a new house with a serving hatch to have shouty, sticky children. I couldn't understand being like that. I'd thought Kimberley was like me. I'd thought she wanted to change the world.

It made me feel like I had to do more, to make up for all the things Kimberley wasn't going to do now. I danced more. I made more friends. And I always tried to speak up when I thought something wasn't fair. All through the lentil-eating nuclear-protesting eighties and the tree-hugging, whale-saving nineties, I never shut up. I didn't want to end up on the wrong side of a serving hatch.

When the factory closed down, everyone went to work in the new call centre, men and women all mixed up together and wearing what they like. Kimberley went there as well, just part time. I saw her a couple of months after she'd started, down the shops. She'd already been promoted to supervisor. We had a good laugh about that. One of her kids was already apprenticed to a builder by then. The other one wanted to be a teacher. It made me think. Maybe there are other ways of changing the world.

I got an invitation in the post today. They're re-opening the factory as an interactive centre to celebrate our industrial heritage. A museum, then. There's a grand opening coming up, with a bar and speeches and a string quartet. There aren't many of the old staff left, so they've just invited the half a dozen of us they could track down. Kimberley as well. They asked us to cut the ribbon on the management staircase. I rang Kimberley straight away so we could decide what to wear. My second call was to the leader of the string quartet to see if she knew the song.

We don't have the platforms and the frosted eyeshadow any more, but I've bought some silver nail polish and we've definitely still got all the moves.

The Aqua Skating Dress
EMMA LEE

When a dress looks gorgeous on a hanger, it's usually impossible to wear. Tori's fingers shook as she eased the ruffled, satiny, aqua dress from the hanger and put it on. She laced her skates.

'You on your own?'

Tori looked up from struggling with the dress's zip to see Elizabeth's mother. Tori nodded. 'It's OK, I can manage.'

'It's always the last inch that's difficult.' Elizabeth's mother moved behind Tori, pushed her hands away and zipped the last section. 'Your mother not here?'

'Thank you.' Tori tried to smile. She found it difficult to raise her arms. The dress was inflexible. 'She's in the audience, probably near the Lord Mayor.' Tori knew 'probably near' wasn't accurate. Her mother hadn't come to drag her home so must have succeeded in getting next to the Mayor.

Elizabeth's mother frowned. 'Most mothers help with changing and make-up. You've done your own?'

Tori nodded. 'I'm better without mum, to be honest.'

'Let me know if you want a hand. Elizabeth's so practised at this, I'm almost redundant. But these costumes are so stiff and tight.' She indicated Tori's dress.

Tori nodded. She didn't think she'd have got the zip done up without help. She tried moving her shoulders, but there was no give in the fabric.

Elizabeth's mother nodded as if Tori had given the right answer to an unspoken question. 'Elizabeth had that too. Sienna had a broken zip. We've had to sew her in. But you're on the skinny side. Go and wait with the others.'

Tori was grateful to move away from scrutiny. She joined the others who were waiting at the rear of the rink. The rink had a third curtained off to create a backstage area. Elizabeth was skating her solo routine, after which the chorus line were to execute a step sequence around the rink before forming a line in front of the curtain to watch the next soloist. They were supposed to be toy dolls who'd come to life during the night.

'I think whoever made these forgot we're not mannequins but actually supposed to skate.' Sienna nudged Tori. 'I can't get my arms above my head and I'm hoping the stitching holds.'

'If Elizabeth's mum did it, you'll be OK.'

'Good point. She'll have had plenty of practice with emergency repairs with her golden girl.'

Tori stifled a giggle, 'Don't be mean. Elizabeth's talented.'

'Yeah, but we don't need to be reminded every five minutes.'

'Her mum's not that bad.'

Sienna tugged at her dress, trying to create space to breathe. 'I wish, sometimes, she wasn't so nice. It should be easy to hate Elizabeth, but it isn't.'

Tori scanned the skaters backstage. 'Have you seen Jacob?'

'Rumour has it you're being paired.'

Tori shrugged.

'You'd look cute together.'

'Don't. His mum already has us married with three blond kids.'

'So what's the problem? Can't have been a lover's tiff already.'

'You know I'm not allowed to date.'

The ice show organisers waved the chorus line group onto the ice. The girls skated to the middle of the curtains and waited for the music. Tori focused on the pair of skaters in front of her. As she skated out, she knew Sienna would be looking at the audience but Tori didn't want to look beyond the barrier. Within the restrictions of the dress, she did the best she could. Tori found herself in between Elizabeth, who was supposed to wait with the chorus line after her slot, and Sienna when they took their places in front of the curtains.

'Well done,' said Elizabeth.

Tori couldn't hear any irony or sarcasm. 'You did well too.'

'Your mother was talking with Jacob's coach earlier.'

Tori groaned inwardly. 'I can imagine.'

'But you and Jacob would be good together. You're both technically good but you've got the musical flair he hasn't.'

'I think I've been embarrassed enough for one night.' Tori was relieved when Jacob skated out to take his place.

'Don't you think?' Elizabeth's whisper was loud enough to hear.

'I don't know.'

'You must know whether you want to skate with him or not.'

'It's not my decision.'

Elizabeth turned her head. 'But what do you want?'

'I don't know.' Tori didn't know how to explain.

'I don't know why your mother's so set against it. Pairing gives you both a chance at the competitions. You know she tried to get you a solo spot when no one gets a solo spot when they first do an ice show.'

'I know. But you try telling my mother.' Tori glanced down at her second hand boots she'd spent hours polishing so they'd look a bit less battered. She looked up again when Jacob's routine brought him closer to the curtained area of the rink. Once he'd finished, there was another group routine during which Elizabeth, Jacob and the chorus line were to leave the stage area and return to the changing rooms.

Tori needed Sienna to help unzip the dress. She almost envied that Sienna had to wait to be unstitched while she changed back into her jeans and sweater, both hand-me-downs from a neighbour. She wasn't ready to go and find her mother so slipped out of the changing room and stood in an alcove where she could see the rink. Her mother hadn't given her instructions on when to join her again, so Tori thought she might get away with waiting until the skating had finished.

'They ought to rename this Tori's spot.'

Tori recognised Jacob's voice so didn't bother looking up to confirm it was him.

'I heard about the costume issues.'

Tori sighed.

'I think my coach is giving your mother a deadline.'

'Good luck with that,' Tori said. 'I know, that sounds harsh, but I don't think she'll shift. My coach has already had a go.'

'Tori…'

Tori looked up.

Jacob's blond hair and blue eyes mirrored her own. He'd changed into jeans and tee shirt with a checked shirt worn as a jacket. She knew under the casual fit, there was a toned, muscular body. He wasn't smiling or laughing at her. He waited.

'Yeah.' She picked at a seam on her jeans.

'Do you ever wear anything new?'

'What's with all the questions?'

'Sorry. Mum wanted to know what dress size you were but Elizabeth's mum said the labels had been cut from your clothes. The woman who made the costumes guessed, but I think she guessed wrong for all of you.'

'She didn't guess wrong. She used the wrong fabric.'

'You're dodging the question. You never seem to wear anything you're comfortable in.'

'I guess not. Your mum makes your outfits?'

Jacob nodded. 'It's OK wearing anything to practise in, but for a competition it makes a difference if what you're wearing fits properly.'

'You know, you haven't insulted me yet.' Tori tried to change the subject. She knew he was right but her mother made her make do with second hand. The ice show had been her first chance to wear something made for her and it had still been uncomfortable. She looked at him and saw sympathy rather than pity.

'I need you fit to skate. I need you confident. Not the scared little rabbit who hides in Tori's spot as soon as she's off the ice. I know it's not your fault, but pairing up just might make things a bit better.'

'I know.' Tori softened her voice.

'What do you think your mum will say?'

As if on cue, Tori heard her mother's voice from the changing rooms, but too muffled to make out the words.

Jacob nodded.

Tori slipped through the toilets to get back to the changing rooms. Elizabeth's mother was standing on one side of a bench near Tori's bags, her mouth forming a smile but her eyes wide and eyebrows raised.

'Of course Jacob might look like a junior champion, but my Tori can do better and she should go it alone. Tonight proved that. The chorus line looked wooden, every one of them. It was embarrassing. And those dresses were so pretty. I said from the beginning, Tori should have had her own solo, not be pushed into a group routine.'

'The dresses had no give in them. None of the chorus line could raise their arms…'

'Nonsense. The skaters should have done better. I kept Tori out of the show deliberately but she begged me to take part in this one. I shouldn't have relented. I was right. Tori!' Tori's mother turned and strode out.

'I'm sorry,' Tori said to Elizabeth's mother. 'She's…'

'Impossible.' Elizabeth's mother helped Tori gather her things. 'I hope you're back for tomorrow night. We'll understand if you're not.'

'I hope so too.' Tori hesitated. She blinked rapidly for a few moments. 'I'm sorry.' She scurried out.

'That coach spoke to me again. It seems he's some pretty grand plans. But pretty grand plans cost more than a pretty penny.' Tori's mother spoke as she walked.

All Tori registered was that they weren't heading for the exit. She felt as if she'd been thrown in the air but not high enough to complete her axel so there was little she could do but land in a twisted heap and skid across the ice.

Her mother reached the seating area reserved for the Mayor, who was in conversation with Jacob's coach.

'My daughter, the skater.'

Tori nodded and smiled on cue.

'She gets her musicality from me, you know. She's a rising star.'

'Yes,' Jacob's coach said.

Tori noticed the exchanged glances between the coach and the Mayor.

'We hope to take our two rising stars to the junior championships,' continued the coach.

The Mayor nodded.

'I trust this was one of your less boring engagements.' Tori's mother said.

Tori got what the coach was trying to do: float the idea of Jacob and her pairing in front of the Mayor so her mother couldn't refuse, but her mother was slipperier than a blunt pair of blades. If she didn't want something to happen, it wouldn't. Tori felt torn. Part of her wanted to be with Jacob and the kindness of Jacob's mother but part of her felt it would highlight what she didn't have and make her feel its loss more keenly. Right now, she wanted to melt into the rubber matting.

'I've been hearing good things,' said the Mayor.

Tori guessed he was being kind.

Jacob's coach smiled. 'We start work next week.'

Tori's mother said something she couldn't hear and the Mayor turned his attention away.

Tori dashed for her alcove.

Jacob caught her. 'Hey, it's OK, really it's OK.'

She heard his voice and leant against him. She straightened but he kept his arm around her waist. 'It's OK now.'

'You still look pale. You want this, right?'

'I don't know.' She looked up at him but only saw concern where she'd expected a mocking grin.

'Why? You know you're better than the chorus line. You won't screw up because you won't let your partner down.'

'I don't know if it's what I want.'

Jacob waited.

'I get told what I want. I get dressed in stuff that doesn't suit me. Giving me a choice backfires because I always choose wrong.' Tori bit her lip.

'No. It's like you need an obstacle to work against. Like your costume. You were the best in the chorus line because the costume was too stiff but you found a way to make it work. If the costume had been perfect, you'd have screwed up. Luckily, I'm not perfect. You need to make me that dress. That sounded wrong. I know that sounded wrong. I didn't mean it to come out like that. But I think you know what I mean.'

She nodded.

'You've lost your voice. Say something. Let me know you understand.'

'I understand. I need to find something that fits and feels good.' She dabbed at her cheeks with her sleeve, careful not to smudge her make-up.

'Think of it as making me look good.'

Despite herself, she smiled. Jacob didn't need any help in looking good.

'It was you who gave me the idea, you know.'

'I don't.'

'Yeah. Watching you in your costume on for the first time. Sienna and Elizabeth and the others fidgeted, pulled the seams, waved their arms and complained about the wrong material. You expected it to be a bad fit. I look at your mother. She looks good when someone's paying her attention, but fidgets and complains when the spotlight's on someone else. My coach is going to tell her we'll have solo routines at the next ice show.'

'But we won't?'

'We could. But the organisers might run out of time. But if it looks to her as if she's going to be the mother of the star of the show… You've stopped shaking.'

Tori shifted her weight so she was standing without leaning against Jacob. 'I think I'm going to ask if I can keep the aqua dress.' She tried to smile. It would be OK on the ice where the lights blanked out the audience so all she had to focus on was the music, repeating a routine until muscle memory kicked in and she didn't even have to think. But, no matter how long she was on the rink, she still had to come off at some point.

'Think how well you skate with that stupid dress on and in second hand boots, scared of putting a foot wrong. How much better could you skate in a costume that fitted with someone supporting you?' Jacob's voice was low and quiet so only she could hear.

'What if I'm not good enough?' She wanted the comfort of crying but her tears wouldn't come.

'Then I'd drop you in a death spiral. But you'd get up and carry on skating.'

Tori gasped: if a skater's hand slipped while their partner was in the spiral, the angle and speed meant the risk of a broken neck. 'I'd be a ghost.'

'No, you're already a ghost. You need some substance or a cheerleader.'

Tori realised her gaze had dropped to the floor. She looked up at Jacob and saw his concerned expression.

'What do you want, Tori?'

She bit her lip. Now wasn't the time for a default "don't know" but what did she want?

'What feels right. Ice beneath my blades.'

THE LEICESTER WRITES SHORT STORY PRIZE 2019

Promises
THOMAS MORGAN

My mother died a couple of days ago. She was seventy-eight years old. She left me two hideous mint green chairs. I don't want them – why would I? They're just awful, and I don't have the room for two ugly chairs in my flat. But my mother made me promise not to throw them away.

'Do you promise?' she said.

'Yes, yes. I promise,' I said.

That was the last conversation I had with my mother.

I picked them up yesterday morning. On my way back to my flat, I walked past a skip that sat in someone's driveway. I thought about tossing the chairs in that skip. Then I wouldn't have to lug them to the tip. Someone might even want them. Maybe a homeless person could make use of the chairs. Giving them to a homeless person would be a nice thing to do – they get something, and I get something. Everybody wins.

I didn't go through with it in the end.

I called my older brother Terry and asked if he wanted them.

'No chance,' he said.

'Come on,' I said. 'I don't want them. I haven't got the room.'

'I don't want them, either,' he said. 'Anyway, I don't think you should throw them away.'

'But I don't want them,' I said.

'Do you think I want twelve Wedgewood plates?' he said. 'No, I don't. But I'm keeping them. I made a promise to Mum. It's the right thing to do.'

'Can't we do a swap,' I said. 'I'll take the plates, you take the chairs. That's a pretty reasonable compromise.'

'Goodbye, Matt,' he said, and hung up.

I don't care what Terry says, I thought to myself. I'm getting rid of the chairs.

I called the council to see if they would take them off my hands. I thought I would do the right thing, instead of just leaving them in the car park behind Morrison's.

'What sort of condition are they in?' said the woman from the council. She had a rather deep and raspy voice.

'Why does that matter?' I said. 'You're getting two free chairs here. The condition shouldn't matter.'

'Condition is very important to us,' she said. 'We need to know this information. Otherwise we won't be able to move forward with the collection.'

'They're in good condition,' I said. 'There's a mark underneath one of the chairs, but other than that, they're in good order.'

'What kind of mark?' she said.

'I don't know,' I said. 'It looks like pen. Possibly permanent marker.'

'Hmm...' she said. 'It would be better if it didn't have the mark.'

'Well, in an ideal world, they would be in better condition,' I said. 'But they've been in my family for decades.'

'Are you sure you want to get rid of them?' she said. 'Once we've taken them, you won't be able to get them back.'

'Yes, I'm sure,' I said. I was starting to get frustrated with this woman from the council. 'So, when can you come and get them?'

'We can pick them up tomorrow,' she said. 'But it'll cost you forty pounds.'

'Fine,' I said. I wasn't best pleased about having to pay to get rid of the chairs, but I just wanted those ghastly things out of my flat, out of my life.

The council came and took the chairs this morning. Even though I paid forty pounds for the privilege of having two fat men come to my house, eat all of my biscuits, and collect the chairs, I still had to help load them into the van. I thought about saying something – about how I paid to have my chairs taken away, yet I was the one who appeared to be doing all of the work. But I thought better of it.

I watched the two fat men get in the van and take the chairs away. Finally, I thought to myself. I'm free.

I wake up in the middle of the night with a sharp pain in the pit of my stomach. I've never experienced anything like this before. I have the occasional night where sleep eludes me, but it's never been quite like this. The pain is so intense that I have to sit up in bed. As I sit in bed and hold my stomach, I start to think about the chairs. I remember having to sit on one of those chairs on Christmas day. My grandparents on my mother's side would join us for Christmas dinner, but we only had four dining chairs in the house; one for my mother, one for my father, one for my brother, and one for me. My brother and I had to sacrifice our usual chairs – the ones we always sat on – and sit on the mint green monstrosities. I miss those Christmases with my parents. Now it's just my brother and me. We don't get together very often – certainly not for Christmas. He does his thing, I do mine.

Suddenly, I hear my mother's voice in my head.

'Do you promise?' it goes. 'Do you promise?'

I start to think that maybe my brother was right. Maybe I shouldn't have gotten rid of those chairs. Maybe I shouldn't have broken my promise to my mother.

Sometimes, when I have trouble sleeping at night – like I said, it doesn't happen very often, but it does happen now and again – I go to the library. I live just a stone's throw away from my old university campus, and the library is open twenty-four hours a day to students and alumni. It's become a soothing ritual for me. In fact, I've often woken up with my face buried in the history of the Russian church. I sit in the same place every time. It's quiet and out of the way– right on the top floor. I call it my nook.

I choose a book at random from the shelf and make my way up the stairs, up to my nook on the top floor. That's where I see them. I think that I must be dreaming. Surely this must be a dream; it's not possible for my chairs to be in the library. It's just not possible. I walk over and inspect the chairs, looking for that Sharpie mark on the underside of the fabric. It's there all right. I grab a big pile of books from a nearby shelf and place the stack on one of the chairs. I take a seat on the other chair. This way, no-one else can sit on *my* chairs.

I sit there for a few hours and wait for the library to officially open for the day. I look over the railing and see someone take a seat behind the front desk.

'Excuse me,' I say, as I march over. 'I've noticed some new chairs on the first floor. Can you tell me where you got them?'

'I'm not sure,' says the man behind the front desk. He has a big beard and his moustache is curled up at the ends with moustache wax.

'It's just, I think those are my chairs,' I say. 'I sold them to the council. But now I want them back.'

'I'm sorry,' he says. 'They're our chairs now. There's really nothing I can do.'

'What do you mean there's nothing you can do?' I say. 'I'm offering to buy them from you. Tell me what you paid for them and I'll double it. If that's not good enough for you, then I'll triple it. Just name your price.'

The library's security guard walks over. 'Is there a problem here?' he asks.

'No, there's no problem,' I say. 'I'm simply enquiring about the price of your chairs.'

'This is a library, not a furniture store,' he says. 'If you're going to start causing trouble, then I'm going to have to ask you to leave.'

I don't want to leave without my chairs. What if someone ruins them? But I have no choice. I pick up my things and walk out of the library. As I walk down the steps, a thought pops into my head. I'm going to do it, I say to myself. I'm going to get my chairs back.

I wait until Friday night. The library won't be busy on Friday night. Most of the students will be out enjoying themselves and spending all of their money. I've never done anything like this before, but I've seen plenty of television programmes and films involving a heist – a bank job or a rescue mission, that sort of thing. I think I've got a good system. I'm going to walk into that library, go up to the first floor, pick up one of my chairs, and take it down to the basement. Then I'll come back for the other one and repeat the process. Once I have both chairs in the basement, I'll sneak out of the fire exit. I'll be gone before anyone knows what's happened.

I go into the library and walk through the gate, scanning my library card on the card reader. I notice a different security guard sitting behind the security desk. I nod at him; he nods back. I might actually get away with this, I think to myself.

I make my way up the main staircase and onto the first floor. I see both of my chairs in the corner next to a block of computers. I check that the coast is clear and walk over to my chairs. I pick up the one with the Sharpie mark on the underside. As I turn around, I find the security guard standing in front of me.

'Excuse me,' he says. 'What do you think you're doing?'

I freeze.

'Uh...' I say. 'I'm just taking this chair up to the top floor. I usually sit up there, but these chairs are much more comfortable than the ones upstairs. I suffer from lower back pain, and my chiropractor has advised me to sit in chairs such as these if at all possible.'

Did he believe that? I was never that good at lying. Terry would've been able to come up with a better lie than that. Where's Terry when you need him?

'I can't allow you to move furniture around,' he says. 'You'll just have to sit here instead.'

I think about making a run for it with the chair. At least I'll have one of the chairs. That's got to count for something – surely that's got to count for *something*.

'Okay,' I say. 'I'll put it back. I promise.'

My chairs have been gone for almost a year now. Every now and then, when I can't sleep at night, I go to the library, sit on those chairs, and think about my mother.

THE LEICESTER WRITES SHORT STORY PRIZE 2019

Five Strong Colours
DONNA BROWN

Living off the land is hard, and Yan was only seventeen. The unceasing threat of drought weighted heavy on his heart. Each night the sky rose mauve above the thick walls of his tent, then faded to black before curdling to amber at dawn, and each night he dreamt of the great city three hundred miles below his home on the high plateau. In his mind's eye, its lights shone brighter than any star in the clear night sky, and its silky voice whispered the same mantra over and over. *Here you will find adventure, the thrill of the forbidden, the chance of glory. Here you will find money. Here you will find life.*

Yan listened carefully and knew it to be true. The city had wound the intricate map of its broad streets, gracious canals and twisting, turning alleys so tightly about him that he was snared more surely than any prince caught fast in a fairy-tale wood. So, at last, he told his mother and grandfather that he, like his brothers before him, would leave.

Yan was not, however, a heartless boy. Even at seventeen, with the world before him and the life of a nomad shimmering into unreality, he found it hard to stand and watch his mother prepare their final meal beneath a line of coloured flags that tore and snapped in the wind. It was a thin broth with dried meat and barley, and as he bent to help her, the wind wicked the tears away from his eyes. She did not look up, except to turn her face into that drying, chapping wind, but they talked, after a fashion, and her questions about the luggage and journey jarred at his brain, whilst the answers gutted in his throat as he absently regarded the repeating blue, white, red, green and yellow pattern of the flags.

A great part of him – the man – longed to set out, aim for the horizon, and put the pain of leaving behind him. The child in him wanted only to be free from the promise of greater things and the expectation of better things, and to sit contented whilst his mother cooked, washed, swept and mended, and the bells around the sheep's necks softly rang. But when the man comes up against the child, the man generally wins, so Yan shouldered his pack and left.

He did not look back more than once, but once was enough because he was not a hard-hearted boy, just ambitious. His mother waved, her arm swinging back and forth like a metronome whilst her face twisted in pain. His grandfather simply stood and watched him go. *Enough*. Yan closed his eyes and let the chapping wind burn across his cheeks as he bid them a silent goodbye, then pictured the city ahead. He promised himself that he would send money home: all the money he could earn if he worked hard, and Yan knew how to work hard – the high plateau could be an unforgiving place.

Many days passed. Yan walked until the familiar plains gave way to valleys lined with conifer and cut by tumbling water. Each night he lay down beneath the stars and pulled the folds of his blanket close. The world around him was changing, and his heart would quail if he let his thoughts run, but walking all day makes for a tired body, so Yan thought little and slept well.

With sore feet and a trembling heart, he eventually arrived on the outskirts of the city. It was not as he had expected. Straggling huts created a desultory line – the ragged hem of a great town – and green gave way to mud. There seemed nowhere to stop, so Yan kept walking. His mind was troubled by what he saw in the faces of the women and children – there was no welcome there, just the dullness that is conjured by drudgery – but he was young, and he pushed the images firmly aside. Ahead, the heart of the city shone slate grey, with the sun's rays beating out a heat that felt more relentless than the wind on the high ground.

Yan walked all day, and the mud eventually gave way to concrete, towering on either side of him like granite cliffs. Exhausted, he sat down at the crossroads of two long, straight streets. He had the address of his brothers, but he had no map, so he did not know how to find their street. He had been sitting for all of a minute when a man came towards him waving his hands. Angry. Yan could not understand the man's dialect, but the intent was clear. *Move on.* Yan looked down and suddenly realised how dirty he was, how roughly fashioned his clothes were and how soiled they were from the journey – how he smelt. He shuffled away, the man's high-pitched imperatives still ringing in his ears.

As Yan walked, rain began to fall. It was the first rain Yan had felt that summer, for the high plateau had become dry, as if the land itself wanted to push the people away and be left alone to quietly decay into desert. Yan turned his face to the sky and let the water run down his cheeks, washing off the dirt of the road. Then he licked the moisture from his chapped lips and went to find his brothers.

Years flowed by, as only years can. Yan worked, and the seventeen-year-old boy grew a beard and forgot to look up at the sky. He worked hard, willingly spending his strength each day, but his lips remained chapped and his pockets remained empty. What little he and his brothers could spare, they sent to their mother and grandfather. When it rained – and in the city it often rained – water ran away across the concrete as it sought a place to sink into the earth. It made Yan recall the rolling plains and the great sky that arced above them – the pale canvas that framed those endless miles. *Could that be the same sky as this pinched expanse of grey that he saw through the tiny windowpane of their shared room? Was this water that flushed down the foul streets the same water that sparkled in the great blue lake when the midday sun winked overhead?* Yan was usually too weary to seek answers to these questions, and others that troubled his heart.

One day the news came that Yan's grandfather had died. Old news already when it reached them. They were to expect his mother soon. Yan walking out into the narrow street and pulled a few dull coins from his pocket. He let them fall into the dirt at his feet. They were worth nothing now. His eyes sought out the meagre sky, framed by regiments of dirty bricks. He wanted to weep, but the tears would not come. At last he asked himself that final question: the one that had been crouching unformed for years in the hollowness that had grown inside him. *Where is the love?*

*

A year later, Yan sat beside his tent, squinting as the wind whipped across his face, even thought it was hidden deep within the fir trim of his hood. He thought of the city, with its tight grey streets and endless rain, then he thought of his grandfather and realised that he was glad that at least the old man had never seen that place or known that the drought would never end.

Three years had passed now on the high ground, and there had been no proper rain. The desert was coming, he mused, then started in surprise as a drop of water landed at his feet. It remained spherical for a moment, before flattening, then, with infinite slowness, sank away into the parched earth.

He watched the darkness of its imprint fade, then turned his face towards the sky; it was pale blue and near cloudless. *Could it have been a raindrop?* He wiped his eyes, and the dust from his hands made them sting. *Perhaps it had been a tear?* One single tear wrung out of him at last, after all these long years. He had not cried since that day he had walked away – seventeen years old, and with every thought and idea new and ready to unfurl inside him like the fronds of a fern in the springtime. He blinked, and small rivers of tears sprang forth and rolled down his cheeks, washing away the dirt.

Around him, the sheep huddled together, their thick coats matted with dust, and the bells around their necks ringing half-heartedly as their curled horns softly chinked. Gusts of wind buffeted the hide walls of his tent. Yan narrowed his eyes, blurring the high sandy plateau with its parched and faded grasses, and the sky that stretched across it, until, through his tears, he saw only earth and air. After a few minutes he dried his eyes and rose, patting the nearest sheep roughly on its head, and went inside.

Closing the tent flap carefully behind him, Yan went to the old wooden box that served him, and his mother and grandfather before him, as both table and treasure chest. He removed the cloth that covered it – folding it carefully and setting it to one side – then lifted the lid.

Inside the box many items of clothing, leather and fur jostled for space, but, peeping between the folds of a blanket, he saw primrose yellow, sharp green, then the blue that he loved – a deeper, richer shade than the sky colour. It was the blue that sparkled in the lake that was hidden away beyond the high plateau, amidst the mountains.

He held the first rectangle of cloth, running the fabric between his fingers, observing its newness. Next, he pulled the string attached to the cloth, and out came white – like the cumulus clouds – then red, next green, and finally yellow. A few moments later, Yan sat with a string of coloured flags stretched out on the cloth, and his chapped lips relaxing into an unfamiliar smile.

Humming quietly to himself, he closed the box, bundled up the flags, replaced the cloth and went back outside. Immediately the wind silenced him, scratching his face with grit. Watched by the sheep, he tied one end of the string to a pole adjacent to the tent, before draping the flags around its hide walls, and fastening the other end to its apex.

Then he sat down amongst the sheep, waiting for his mother and brothers to come home. As he waited, he listened to the new flags snapping in the wind. Blue, white, red, green, yellow. Peace began to fill the hollow he had carried inside himself for so long, and his sorrow rested on the back of the desert wind.

THE LEICESTER WRITES SHORT STORY PRIZE 2019

Asylum
PATRICIA M. OSBORNE

A clock ticks loudly. A smell – disinfectant? My fingertips tingle. A bright light. Rows of yellow teeth appear an inch from my face. The stench of stale tobacco makes me want to vomit.

I try to move but remain rigid. A young woman, dressed in blue with a white apron and hat, touches my shoulder. She smiles. My head is cold and sticky. It hurts. Someone's tugging my hair. My whole body vibrates but I remain restrained in the demon's trap. I squeeze my eyes shut.

When I open my eyes again I'm alone. I glance around the white-walled room but there's nothing to see. Just the narrow bed I'm lying on and a window that's too high to reach. Footsteps. My heartbeat quickens. I rub my sore wrists. Someone outside turns a key, it grinds, the handle lowers. The girl from the dark chamber faces me. She smiles. I shiver.

'Good morning Olivia. I'm Nurse Simms.'

Olivia, is that me?

'Doctor says you can go outside for a short while. Shall we?'

I follow her.

The outside door opens. I stumble down the wide steps and take in the cloudless blue sky and various shades of green. My nose tickles from the scent of roses. I gaze at my reflection in the glass of the nearside building. A young woman with straggly hair stares back. Did I always look so bedraggled?

I hear music. On moving closer I recognise the sound as coming from a piano. Glancing down at my long fingers, I imagine them gliding over the black and white keys.

'Do you play?' Nurse asks.

'I don't remember.'

'When you're feeling better, you can join the group session.'

Am I ill?

We walk towards cedar and yellow-green bushes. Blackbirds, crows and blue-tits flit from tree to tree. Crows shriek, blackbirds and blue-tits tweet and trill. I close my eyes.

Suddenly a bang. There it goes again. Bang. I cup my ears.

'It's fine, Olivia.' Nurse leads me to a bench. 'It's nothing to worry about. It's only thunder.'

I need to get away. I strike her. She stumbles and raises both arms in front of her face. A doctor and two muscular male attendants run from the house. They hold me down.

'Plea...se. No..., plea...se.' A large phial of liquid flashes in the sunlight. I thrash my arms. Fluid surges through my veins.

When I wake my head throbs. I can't move. My chest hammers. Gasping for breath, I manage to ease myself up on the hard mattress and look around. I don't see a window. Nothing to see except white padded walls.

The next thing I know Nurse is stripping the tight jacket away.

'Olivia, you have a visitor. It's your sister.'

My sister. I don't remember a sister. Nurse guides me outside. I stare into space, shuffling one foot in front of the other along the stone floor. The cold beneath my feet makes me shudder as we walk out of the building and down the steps. It's cooler than last time I went outside. There's no blue sky, only a white sheet hovering in the air. Distant trees blanched with a silvery mist.

A young, dark haired woman walks towards me. She looks elegant in her tight skirt suit, not dowdy like me in this shabby dress. She hugs me, I drop my shoulders. She raises her eyebrows. 'Hello Olivia, it's me, Emily? Do you remember me?'

Her hands shake. 'Do you know why you're here?'

I don't know why I'm here. I don't know you, and I don't know who I am. All I know is I'm in Hell.

'Do you remember your husband, James?'

I look up at the trees. A thunderstorm. I remember thunder. A man shouting. I hold my throat. I open my mouth to speak but no sound is released. Emily wraps her arms around me.

'I don't remember,' I whisper, 'I don't remember. If you're my sister, please get me out of here. They strap me to a bed, put rods on my head and make me shake and screech with pain, then darkness.'

Emily strokes my face. 'That must be the treatment.'

I grab her arm. 'Please, please, take me home.'

She pats my hand. 'I'm sorry Olivia but I can't. You need to stay in hospital. You're not well.'

I'm not well. I don't remember.

Emily leads me to the bench. 'Sit here whilst I go and organise tea. I won't be long.'

She climbs the steps and stops to talk to Nurse. They close the door behind them. They're conspiring against me. I hold up my dress so not to trip up and run into the thick haze. The doctor and two male wardens race towards me. I turn and head for the trees. Sweat beads drip from my forehead. I must get away. Heavy footfalls. I run faster but slip. Hands grab me. Hands pull me. My kicks and screams are futile, no one listens or comes to my aid. They're all out to get me.

I don't remember how I got here but I recognise the white padded walls. My arms are chained by the prison jacket, it prevents me from covering my ears to quieten the voices. Pictures, there are pictures too. A man. James? James staggers, James sways, James shouting. His whisky breath makes me heave. Crockery crashes to the floor. Food splats across the wall. My face stings. James is punching me. Fluid swills around my mouth. It tastes salty. He presses his fingers on my throat. I must make him stop. A knife? It's in my hands. Blood? More blood, we're covered in blood.

Whispering. I hear whispering. They're plotting against me. I sit and rock but still hear them. I hum to drown out their words.

THE LEICESTER WRITES SHORT STORY PRIZE 2019

Social Conditioning
DIANNE BOWN-WILSON

Getting that letter from Art was like having a piece of shit posted through your letterbox. You can see straight-off what it is, but for a while disbelief freezes your emotions. All you can think is, How can this be?

I hadn't seen Art for twenty years. We used to be best friends, inseparable. I was married to Judy then and he was with Linda. We'd been at school together, worked in the same place, and were always up for a laugh.

When I read the letter, hands shaking, I learnt that things had changed. *Linda and I split in 2005. A couple of years ago I got hitched again to Mel. She died at the end of last year.*

His handwriting had never been great and the words on the page were awkwardly formed. It looked as though it'd taken him effort to write; it took me considerable effort to read.

It's taken me a long time to find you and I guess that until I hear back, I can't be sure I have. It's been a while, a lot of water under the bridge, but if this does get to you I need you to know that I really could use a little support right now. It's hard being alone and the old ticker's not great. Don't get me wrong, I'm not after money, just a cuppa and a chat.

'Who's that from?' Elaine appeared in the kitchen doorway. 'Anyone I know?'

'No. Just someone from years back.'

'Oh?'

'He's tracked me down. Wants to come and visit - but that's not going to happen. There's a reason you lose touch with people and in this case it's a good one.'

'Sure, if that's the way you feel. Though it can be good seeing old friends again.'

'Not this time.'

I tore the letter into pieces and put it in the kitchen bin. There are old friends and then, there's Art. Another twenty years' water under the bridge still wouldn't be enough.

Ten days later, home from the bowling club, I opened the front door to an odour so immediately recognisable I almost gagged. Surely not…

Then I heard his voice.

Art.

Him and his puke-inducing aftershave in my house, my home, my Englishman's bloody castle.

The bastard.

'Phil - look who's here.' Elaine pulled me into the sitting room. There was a tightness about her eyes.

'Mate. Look at you!' Art raised a hand and grinned. An empty cup and plate on the coffee table confirmed he'd been here a while.

'I'll make more tea,' Elaine said, and vanished.

I walked over to the fireplace. My mind was racing with a million things I might say but all I could come out with was, 'What a surprise.'

It was hard to recognise the man in front of me as the Art I'd known. Back then, he'd been a snappy dresser, sleek as an otter, as proud of himself as his idol, George Best. Now, wrinkled and balding with stubble like mould, he seemed to be crumbling, decayed.

'Yeah, sorry mate. I wrote to you, but when I got no answer I wasn't sure what to think so I figured I'd check out whether I'd got the right gaff. And I'm glad I did. Lovely place you've got here, and Elaine and me have been having a good old chat!'

My jaw tightened. The essence of him hadn't changed but, evidently, neither had I. Despite how much I loathed him I was prepared to let him sit there, burbling, just as if we were still best friends.

#

Twenty years ago:

'Mate! What you doing here?' He stands framed in the front doorway of his house; it's Sunday morning, not yet nine o'clock.

'You know why. You know what you've done.'

He raises his eyebrows, feigning puzzlement. 'Something wrong?'

'WRONG? You don't know the meaning of the word.'

Unfazed, he leans against the door jamb. 'Aw come on, that's a bit strong. If it's what I think you're on about, there's no need to get so aerated. It was just a bit of fun, nothing serious.'

Nothing serious! The memory blazes inside my brain like a Piccadilly Circus neon billboard: him pressed up against her, his leg between her thighs, hands and mouth…

Helplessness threatens to overwhelm me but I force out the words. 'Don't you ever, ever, go near her again, you scum. And from now on, outside of work, you're dead to me; we're no longer friends!'

He shrugs, and as I turn away he laughs softly, 'What a prick.'

#

Social conditioning, they call it, the process by which we're trained to exhibit socially-acceptable behaviours and emotional reactions. I learnt this from Monica, the psychologist I saw after Judy and I broke up.

Throughout our married life she always said I was too controlled, downright weak. 'What would it take for you to man up and hit back?' she'd yell, but I never replied.

I didn't know.

I never have.

After the business with Art and all the problems we had with Lily – during which Judy and I grew further and further apart - I found myself suffering panic attacks, being suffocated by my own impassiveness.

'How we are as adults reflects how we were raised,' Monica said, and I thought of my meek yet overbearing parents, who wanted nothing more than for their boy to get on, and of Art's, who amidst the hurly-burly of their knockabout existence barely seemed to register he was theirs. Now, as a parent myself, I didn't know how to behave.

When I told Monica about Art and our unlikely friendship she said, 'Perhaps, subconsciously, you saw it as a way to rebel.'

When I told her about what he'd done and how I reacted she said, 'Don't blame yourself. Many of us are conditioned to be non-confrontational, we exact retribution in different ways.'

#

Seeing Monica helped, but she wasn't a magician, so nothing about me fundamentally changed. That's why Art was now sitting in my easy chair instead of being sprawled outside on the pavement.

Not that I was a complete pushover. After Elaine brought more tea, Art told us about his current circumstances, recounting every detail of Mel's death and how, without her, he was finding life a challenge. I might have sympathised, but I didn't say a word.

'Problems with all the probate and stuff now,' he said, 'Temporary financial problems, but that'll all get sorted. I do miss her though, love of my life she was.' Elaine smiled politely.

'You know, I was surprised to hear that you and Judy split, though now I've met Elaine I can see why…' He winked. 'And your girl?'

'Lily's fine. Married, kids.' It was all he needed to know. I had no intention of discussing any aspect of my life with him; it was time he left.

'So where are you staying tonight – presumably you're not driving all the way back?'

'Good question, mate. I was so keen on getting here, not knowing what I'd find, that I haven't got anything sorted.'

'Fine. I can point you in the direction of plenty of B&Bs though I suggest you find somewhere soon or you'll be driving about in the dark.'

'True.' He glanced at the clock. 'Guess I'd better be off then.' He struggled out of the chair, wincing. 'All seizes up a bit these days if I'm sitting about – those bits that haven't completely given up already!' he barked a laugh. Neither Elaine nor I reacted.

At the front door, he turned. 'Well, I know we've hardly spent any time together but I have to say it's been just like old times. Great to see you, mate, and you, too, Elaine. Must meet up again soon.'

'Sure.' I was aware he didn't have my phone number and prayed he wouldn't ask for it. Hell would have to freeze over before I'd have him in my house again.

After we watched him hobble down the path, he drove away in a battered transit van and the moment he vanished from sight we closed the door.

I spoke first. 'The cheek of him, coming here like that.'

Elaine looked uncertain. 'Presumably it was him who wrote to you; do you want to tell me about it?'

'No. We had a falling out and I told him he was dead to me. Nothing's changed.'

'Well, I doubt we've seen the last of him. My money's on him dropping by again tomorrow.'

'We'd better make sure we're out, then. Maybe a drive and a nice lunch somewhere?'

'Sounds good,' she smiled. 'For now, I could murder a drink.'

#

Unfortunately, Elaine lost her bet. Only an hour or so later, the doorbell rang. We looked at each other.

'Man, what can I say? You won't believe what's happened. I got to a B&B, looked for my wallet, and found I've either lost it or left it at home. Of course, they wouldn't let me stay there without paying so I'm completely up the creek. You haven't found it here, have you?'

'No,' said Elaine.

For a moment, he seemed to sway, then clutched the doorframe for support. From the set of his mouth it seemed as if he might be in pain.

'Are you alright?' I had to force the words out. I didn't care how he was but, equally, I didn't want him collapsing on my doorstep.

'Yeah, yeah. Ticker's not too good, as I think I may have said. Plays me up a bit sometimes. I …' He seemed to wince again.

'Perhaps you'd better come in.'

Fairly smartly, all things considered, he followed us back to the sitting room where he collapsed into the same chair – my chair – that he'd only recently vacated.

Elaine left us, returning a few moments later with a glass of water. During her absence neither Art nor I said anything.

'Thanks, pet,' he mumbled, as she placed it in front of him.

Elaine looked into my eyes and inclined her head ever so slightly: We need to talk, now.

'Just relax, Art,' she said. 'We'll be back in a minute.'

In the kitchen, she didn't mince her words. 'Look, I know you don't like him, but he's not looking in great shape and he hasn't got any money. I wouldn't feel happy about him driving, so unless he stays here, you're going to have to get a taxi to get him back to the B&B – you've been drinking so you can't drive - then pay for his room, and get him something to eat from somewhere. Surely it's just easier to let him stay here and get rid of him in the morning?'

She was right, she usually is, and although every molecule of my being was screaming NO! I couldn't think of what else to do. We were trapped and probably tricked, but despite my suspicions, I couldn't be sure. What if he wasn't acting and after I threw him out he dropped dead in the street?

'Look it's only for one night. Let's go and tell him.'

I followed Elaine back to the sitting room, my heart pounding with frustration.

#

Oh he played us, virtuoso style. And what was worse, he knew that I knew he was doing it.

That first night was low-key: we shared our meal and offered no alcohol, ate with minimal conversation, and cleared the plates away quickly. Elaine went upstairs and returned a few minutes later.

'I've run you a bath, Art' she said firmly, and I knew that this wasn't for his good. There was no way she was having him, unwashed, sullying her spare-bedroom sheets.

'Ah, no need,' Art said.

'No trouble,' said Elaine with that uncompromising touch of steel that had made her so successful in her pre-retirement working life. 'Phil, I'll leave you to show Art around upstairs. Sleep well Art, see you in the morning.'

She ushered us both from the room and a few minutes later, I too wished him a terse goodnight. Already, I was counting the hours until he'd be gone.

But, of course, it wasn't hours.

For the first couple of days he feigned illness: the journey had tired him out. The stress of losing his wallet. The change in the air. The ability to relax after all the grief and tribulations following Mel's death… No, he didn't need a doctor, he knew his old body, it'd soon pass. Of course, he was mortified that he was putting us to so much trouble, but he knew an old mate like me would never let him down, and Elaine was just an angel.

Day three he was better, enough to be up and about, but still not recovered sufficiently to set out on the long drive home. Strong enough for a stroll around the neighbourhood, though – get a bit of the old sea air.

Day four was the same, though he did make noises about 'making tracks tomorrow'. Elaine and I looked at each other. We'd both been too incensed by the whole thing to discuss it on any level other than, When's he going to go, how do we get him out?

That night, over dinner he said he'd been thinking of selling his house and that having strolled around our neighbourhood and looked in a few estate agents' windows, he'd decided it'd be great to come and live near us.

'Wouldn't live in your pockets or anything. You'd probably never see me. But it'd be great to know I've got my old mate and his lovely wife just there in the background. Like family, you are.'

Even before this latest bombshell my nerves were as taut as piano strings. Hatred had kept me awake every night while despair at my own impotence had turned my body into a seething mass of aches and pains. When would there be an end to this bloody game? How could I stop him? I could have it out with him, tell him straight that it wasn't on, but I knew how he'd respond: Phil, man, get real - you can't actually stop me.

Art cut through my thoughts: 'So, I was wondering if you could both put up with me for one more day so I can go and talk to a few estate agents and get things underway. Just the first steps, of course, but once I've done that I can go back home, get things organised there, and I'll be out of your hair.'

Neither of us spoke which, unsurprisingly, he took as agreement. 'Great. Let me help you clear these dishes then, Elaine.'

Teeth clenched so tightly my jaw ached, I left them to it. I needed some air.

As I made for the front door I spotted Art's phone on the hall table. A grubby-looking thing with an unmistakeable purple cover; he must have left it there when he took his coat off. I picked it up, let myself outside and strode round the side of the house to the end of the garden, an area screened from the kitchen by a hedge. Fortunately, it was still just light enough to see and I had no reservations whatsoever about going through his call log.

There were a massive number of unanswered calls, most from the same person, the last only yesterday: Mel.

Was this the same Mel who'd died a few months ago, so he'd told us at length?

There was only one way to find out.

I punched her number into my phone.

She answered within seconds, and it took scarcely any longer to establish that she was indeed Art's wife, fighting fit and as mad as hell. Certainly, she held nothing back in answering my questions, spitting venom at the sound of his name.

'So he's turned up at yours has he? That bastard frittered away everything we had, lied to me, cheated, and rather than face the music, just took off. Well, all I can say is that he'll be stealing from you, too, if he isn't already, so good luck with that.'

There was plenty more I could have asked but after a few minutes of her ranting, I cut our conversation short. The time had come for a showdown.

As I made my way back down the side of the house, brain churning with what I was about to say, I glanced through the kitchen window and froze. There, in the lit-up room, like a scene from an old Music Hall sketch, I watched Art come up close behind Elaine, slip his arms round her and fondle her breasts.

Momentarily, the memory of twenty years earlier blinded me. Our party, that night, the sight of him pawing my fourteen year-old daughter, and me, as now, just watching. Nausea surged in my throat but I breathed it away. I couldn't let it happen again; he'd taken the piss long enough.

But what was this?

Before I had time to move, Elaine whirled round and, judging by his expression, kneed him hard in the groin. I couldn't make out her words but hell, she was shouting mad and he was bent double. She stormed out, leaving him to his pain, while I stood and marvelled.

I let a couple of minutes pass and then knocked on the window.

Art looked toward me, pale and pleading.

I held up his phone. 'Mel', I mouthed.

His anguished face folded even further. Rumbled.

As if hit by a slug of the strong stuff, my head swam with joy. Mel had said she'd be hotfooting it down to reclaim him and from her tone, I was sure she would. And Elaine? What a woman.

As I threw back my head, revelling in victory, my eyes were blinded by fiery shards of setting sun slicing through what had seemed an impenetrably leaden sky.

How can this be?

I couldn't stop laughing.

Corundum Noir
BEV HADDON

Marge steered the Daimler down roads dappled by early afternoon sunlight, as the A33 became the A34 without fuss or fanfare. Helen checked the map again, the long red line that represented the road that seemed straight when you were on it, but looked curved and jagged on the page. She noticed the blue line of the motorway, running along the edge, and carefully refolded the paper to hide it. They'd been travelling for hours, but she couldn't complain; she knew they were going the long way round, and appreciated Marge's tact in not mentioning why.

'It's nice to be out of the house,' Helen had said, three miles ago. But privately she thought it didn't seem much different from sitting at home, except she had swapped the dazzling colours of television for the muted hues of an English winter. All the landscape could be painted by mixing green and brown in the paintbox; sludge, olive, drab. Helen sat in the passenger seat and watched England roll by, its bristly hedgerows festooned with cow parsley. It was impossible to imagine stopping the car and walking across the fields, grasping the weeds. It was just something to see out of a car window, as the fields rolled by like a very long, winding scenery prop.

They played tag with an articulated lorry that had 'Curtains For *You*' in maroon lettering. Marge overtook the behemoth every time the road sloped up; on the down gradient it came thundering past them. They passed a sign that said A34 – caution, low bridge.

'That'll get rid of him,' Marge said, with an air of satisfaction, 'He'll have to turn off.'

The Curtains lorry was in front at that point, and its left-hand indicators came on. Marge pulled alongside it, and pipped her horn in a sarcastic farewell. Helen glanced across, but the driver was expressionless, and a moment later the lorry had vanished down a side road. It seemed to mark a change to the journey; both Helen and Marge shuffled in their seats to get more comfortable.

'There's a thermos in my bag,' said Marge, waving towards the back seat.

Helen reached back, strained and caught hold of the tartan flask. The movement was rather awkward as she was missing a few fingers from her left hand; one couldn't expect to walk away from a three-car motorway pile-up unscathed. She managed to pour herself half a cup of tea, too strong, too sweet but nevertheless welcome. Dear dependable Marge. They had been friends for ever. She sipped the tea whilst she listened to Marge's litany of complaints and admonitions to other drivers. It was what passengers were for, she thought, and wondered what people did who drove alone. Giles had been the same. 'Look at that idiot' he would say, and she would cluck in reproof, staring at a line of cars and wondering which one was the object of his wrath. Poor Giles.

A Jaguar pulled into their lane and Marge had to brake, hard.

'I don't see why I had to go down in person,' she grumbled, not for the first time. 'I hope this shack is worth it.'

'Beach hut, Helen corrected automatically. 'Whatever state it's in, it's worth a bit. Near the pier and handy for the cliff lift? You've fallen on your feet there.'

'I'm glad you're coming with me to help me find the place.'

'Thank you for asking me. It's the first long trip I've taken in real life, since the accident.'

There was a pause, two breaths big, whilst Marge checked the mirror, and attempted to say casually,

'Do you remember any more about it?'

Remember… Helen had tried and tried, but the images slipped away, like the seagulls she and Giles had walked towards on the beach on that last morning. Each time they had grown closer the seagulls hopped further away, only to regroup in the chattering surf. The whorls of memory were buried under layers of scar tissue.

'The police came to see me last week to ask me the same thing, but I couldn't tell them anything about it. I remember getting into the car, and Giles driving onto the motorway, but nothing after that. They've interviewed everyone. They're closing the case. They told me that the driver three cars back hadn't seen anything ahead that could have caused the crash.'

(The occupants of the two cars behind Giles, being, unfortunately, unavailable for comment.)

'The police say the only explanation is that Giles must have swerved to avoid something – an animal, perhaps. Or a bird.'

'They can tell a lot from skid marks,' Marge nodded sagely.

Helen could almost, *almost* see a pigeon flying straight at the windscreen, but then the image faded and she wasn't sure if it was imagination or memory. There were a lot of things she couldn't recall. She could remember the ventilator – the invasive tube down her throat and some panicked shouting and falling into black. Funny that she didn't remember waking up. There must have been police standing around her bed, and doctors with artificially sad faces. Mrs Morley, we have some very bad news…

The car slowed at a roundabout. On the left a bride stood in a field of mud, her brilliant white train unfurling like an incredibly long tongue coated with icing sugar. But the bride's face was straw, turned towards Helen's; just an overdressed scarecrow. There must be a simple explanation – perhaps the dress belonged to someone going through a messy divorce. But Helen couldn't take her eyes off it, couldn't bear to look away until they passed it, just in case the straw face smiled at her.

A tall building loomed to the right, outlined against the sky, a two-dimensional image that wouldn't fool a child. As Helen craned her neck to make sense of it, a car overtook them with a dummy sitting in the passenger seat. It turned to look at them, its blank, slightly green features observing them placidly. Helen waved to it – impelled by the same instinct that made her wave to people on trains. It might be someone she knew looking out through its carefully non-gender-specific face.

'Do you remember Charlotte?' Marge asked. 'Wears a lot of pink, used to come along to WI meetings? I thought about asking her along for the drive. She's been stuck in bed with a dodgy hip since Easter…'

Helen was glad Charlotte hadn't come. That sinking feeling, remembered from childhood, of looking forward to an afternoon arranged with a friend, only to find someone else there – 'I just brought so and so along,' Helen spending the afternoon running after them, catching up.

'…But I didn't know how you felt about having a dummy sitting in the back seat,' Marge went on, 'They give some people the heebie jeebies.'

'I don't mind them,' Helen said truthfully, 'I use them a lot now. Especially since the accident. I used to struggle logging into them.' That moment when you pressed the button and all of a sudden you were seeing through the dummy's eyes. If you thought about what you were actually doing you would trip up, or panic. 'But it's right what people say, you just have to just get going straightaway. Now I stamp my foot a few times and just launch myself forwards.'

Which reminded her of yesterday. Helen wondered if she should say anything. Perhaps not. Only…

'Marge, have you ever wondered if New York is real?'

Marge stared at the road ahead, intent on something invisible to the naked eye.

'Of course it's real. I was only there this morning.' She drifted across to let a van overtake her. She glanced across at Helen's set, frowning face, and sighed.

'Go on then.'

'I wanted that new lipstick –the red so deep it's almost black - Corundum Noir...'

'The one that's only available in Bloomingdales?'

'That's right. I saw it advertised in a magazine and wanted it. So I went to New York yesterday, straight to the store.'

She'd logged herself in to one of the dummies and taken the elevator – she was proud of remembering the word – to the fifth floor, cosmetics and beauty. Other dummies were walking around, examining the products. There were lines around the chest and hips, vaguely suggesting clothing, but as the dummies' sex was indeterminate it didn't really matter. One smiled at her – for all she knew they might be friends. Helen had found the Corundum Noir stand without any problems and picking up one of the testers she painted the dummy's lips with it and examined the result in the mirror, pouting. It was difficult, of course, to tell the overall effect; the dummy's reflection looked back at her, its hair and eyebrows suggested by contours, its face the colour of luminous paint.

'After I bought the lipstick on one of those self-serve tills I had nothing else to do, so I wandered around the shop. I started on the fifth floor and worked down and went all round. And what do you think I found?'

Marge overtook a grey Humber. 'You tell me.'

'There were no people, *anywhere*.'

'Of course not! Bloomingdales is dummy-only – keeps it exclusive. It was the first store to go dummy-only, you remember that.'

Did she? There were a lot of things Helen had forgotten since the accident.

'But they would still need people to work in the shop, to move stock in and out – to clean the dummies.' (Helen was thinking of the lipstick test). 'So I got to thinking, is it even real?'

'And from that – no shop assistants around when you need them – you decided New York is an illusion? Isn't that rather a big step?' Marge chuckled.

'Think about it though,' urged Helen, – 'no-one actually travels to America anymore – it's too expensive. But you can't get in a dummy and make it walk to the Projects or the run-down bits. You can only make it go to the tourist places, like walking up the Statue of Liberty, the Empire State building...'

'Because that's where people want to go!'

'Doesn't that strike you as odd, though?'

'Not as odd as this conversation. Did you get the lipstick, in the end?'

'Oh, the lipstick came,' said Helen. 'Delivered by drone just after I logged out of the dummy.'

'There you are then.'

'But...'

'Here we go!'

'Everything's *wrong*. It's like a dream. Everything sort-of makes sense but when you look at it closely it's all nonsense – drones delivering lipsticks, your aunt leaving you a beach hut in her will, travelling to New York to buy make-up, that scarecrow…'

'What scarecrow?'

Helen's right foot had gone to sleep, she stamped it a few times to get rid of the numbness. She took deep ragged breaths as she voiced her deepest fear. 'What if this is all a dream? What if I'm still on the ventilator? What if I can't wake up?'

Marge smiled at her – a special smile, the smile of a fond parent for an infant who has asked for something impossible. Helen noticed that Marge's lipstick had bled a little around the edges. How had she not noticed that Marge was wearing Corundum Noir? Marge kept smiling and the smile was getting wider, and wider… A lorry was hurtling towards them on the opposite side of the road, with maroon lettering. Helen grabbed the steering wheel and wrenched it a quarter turn to the right.

Thrown clear from the wreckage, Helen sat by the side of the road, nursing scratches from the hedge. She smelt lavender, petrol fumes and an undercurrent of barbecued meat. A person and a dummy knelt over Marge's contorted, twitching corpse with identical expressions of horror. Helen felt the first stirrings of unease. If this was a dream it was a bloody *good* one.

THE LEICESTER WRITES SHORT STORY PRIZE 2019

As Yet Unpublished
BEV HADDON

'Putting together an anthology is an art – you have to get the tonal shifts right – you don't want a farcical story straight after a heart-rending tragedy. You need to keep the reader's interest, you have to entice them into starting the next story, and the next.'

Beth nodded politely, sipping her vending-machine coffee and waiting for him to get to the point.

'This story you've written…' Ned fumbled through the papers in his briefcase.

She sat up straighter. This was why she had arranged to meet him here. Ned was publishing a new anthology and had put out an open call to writers for submissions. She'd sent him a story, he'd emailed her to say he liked it. He was visiting a Book Fair at the weekend, at a local university. Could she meet up, to discuss in more detail?

Ned took out her familiar type-written sheets and exhaled noisily. 'I'm not sure about the title – 'Swallowing Her Pride' – it's kind of nudge-nudge, and it gives away the ending? Also… 2000 words is a bit long, space is always an issue in an anthology, especially now I've got confirmed stories from Stephen and Joe…'

'Yes… it must be so difficult selecting stories.' Not, she suspected, as difficult as writing them in the first place. 'I can shorten it to – say – 1500 words?'

'Make it 1000. And this older man… the publisher. He just comes across as a bit seedy and unsympathetic. And he's too old to be tempted by her, er, offer. Maybe if he was younger – in his forties? And the story would be *much* more convincing if it was written from the young woman's viewpoint.'

'Yes, I could easily rewrite it that way'. She tried not to let her desperation show in her face. At this point she was happy to change the story to a Nordic Noir thriller with a tap-dancing moose.

Ned stroked his on-trend beard thoughtfully, every inch the all-powerful publisher, in his forties but still down with the kids. He had shown her the mocked-up cover for the new anthology, *The Three Stages of Twilig*ht, its classy indigo cover with embossed white lettering. Two stories confirmed but lots of room for others. Room for hers.

'But the main problem I have with your story… is that would any young woman actually go through with this? It's so unlikely.' He looked at her and smiled. 'Convince me. I mean would *any* woman offer, heh, sexual favours just to get a short story published?'

Beth looked around the Dealer's room at the Book Fair – mostly deserted now except for a few assistants putting out books and bottles of water, ready for the afternoon session. Maybe all the writers were off somewhere giving blow jobs to publishers, who knew? What she did know, for sure, was that she wanted to be sitting at one of those tables with a stack of glossy new books all ready to sign. She would sell her soul for Sharpies.

She turned back to him and shifted slightly in her seat to hitch up her skirt.

'I think it's a *totally* believable scenario. I mean, take me for example, I would do anything to have my story included in your anthology…' She stroked the glossy indigo jacket with her index finger. 'To have my story printed next to authors who are household names. And wanting something badly makes people do foolish things…'

He was looking at her with some interest. 'So,' he purred, 'At present you are completely unpublished?' A quick glance down at her body which she was meant to see.

'As yet,' she murmured.

'I've got the key to a room on the second floor,' he said, suddenly business-like.

*****

But that was then, and now here is Beth sitting in a bookshop, signing copies of 'Andromeda's Curse', the fourth book in her successful 'Andromeda' series, and fielding questions from fans about the ongoing love triangle with Brad (dark, brooding, complex) and Tristan (redhead, sexy, no discernible moral compass.)

'No, I can't tell you who she will choose in the end; you'll have to keep reading!' (Quite frankly it doesn't matter much to Beth. Perhaps she would toss a coin.)

She writes a dedication for Carole-with-an-e, then poses for a selfie, glancing at the queue that still snakes around the corner. Next in the line is a young guy in an official Team Tristan t-shirt. Glad to see people are buying the merchandise. He hands her a book to sign but it isn't an Andromeda book – he waits for her to recognise it. Of course she recognises it; it's the book containing her first published story.

'Wow, how did you to track this one down?' she says, after taking a second to collect herself. 'It's been out of print for years.'

'I found it in a charity shop, recognised your name. Cool story! Could you make it out, to Liam?'

She tastes bile at the back of her throat, glad she's looking down so he can't see her face. She searches through the book until she finds the blank half page, opposite the scene where a publisher gets castrated with cheese wire. She writes a dedication, then signs so hard she nearly goes through the paper. Seeing the book brings it all back; how she had shortened her story, retitled it 'As Yet Unpublished', and rewritten it from the woman's point of view; how she had sent Ned the amended 1000 word story, and received a brief acknowledgment; how she had dashed to Waterstones on the day *The Three Stages of Twilight* was published, and picked up her five pre-ordered copies for family and friends, leafing through the book, searching, searching for her story…

She breathes, forces a smile and hands back the bubble gum-pink edition of *Proud Flesh – Feminist Horror Stories*, to its owner.

Because *As Yet Unpublished* had lived up to its name; although she had given Ned 1000 words of polished prose (and the rest) it turned out that Beth had nothing in print, as she had nothing in writing.

Le Petit Oiseau
SARA HODGKINSON

The face of the little bird was burned now into her memory: he had clocked her, frozen, then cocked his head quizzically - searching, perhaps, for an explanation of the scene before him. She had eyed him suspiciously, as though he might betray the event he had just witnessed to another. But he was only a bird. And birds don't often testify to murder. Still, the look he had given Janine as she had rolled Camille's lifeless body into the Seine had stayed with her, and the thought of it made her shudder as she strolled slowly back into central Paris to resume her day.

Camille hadn't been a terrible friend - at least not in the beginning. She had fallen into Janine's life one sunny spring morning on rue de Passy as the pair clashed clumsily in the doorway of Sephora. Janine had spilled her froth-laden cappuccino and Camille had offered to replace it by way of an apology, whisking them both off to a nearby patisserie where they had unexpectedly bonded over caffeine and warm pain au chocolat. A shared love of Balenciaga and Christian Louboutin had seen their friendship blossom and the two were soon regular features on the Champs Elysees. They would shop arm-in-arm for couture designs on their lunch breaks, sip ice-cold Veuve Clicquot on Friday evenings after work, and divulge the latest Paris gossip over long Saturday brunches of exquisite tartines.

Janine hadn't actively kept Camille from Arnaud, yet in hindsight she wondered if the reluctance in her gut to introduce The Friend to The Lover may have been a subconscious reading of the future. The moment Arnaud had laid eyes on Camille, Janine knew that she had made a mistake in bringing the two together. And she knew that there would, undoubtedly, be trouble. It had been as plain as the moon in a clear midnight sky: Arnaud had fallen for Janine's new companion, hopelessly, wholly and completely.

Camille - for her part - gave little away, the initial infatuation of Janine's *amour* appearing one-sided and unrequited in its blatant yet unmistakable intrusion on a hitherto thriving relationship. Though by the time the leaves began to blanket the streets of Paris in patchwork technicolour, Janine could recognise the scent of deceit in her newfound friend.

Confirmation of the pair's betrayal had come in the form of a receipt - paper proof of precious moments stolen together in a tiny bistro far from any of Janine's usual haunts. A whispered phone call overheard in the dim light of dawn had solidified the reality of this deviant and most devastating of dalliances. Janine tailed the two traitors the very next time they met, pursuing them covertly but with a dogged determination to view with her own eyes the disintegration of a life she had planned so meticulously in her mind. She came upon them outside a backstreet brasserie - the vision of a regular couple awaiting their steak, huddled quietly over a carafe of merlot at a modest candlelit table. Janine had retreated into the shadows to maintain her cover, and then, eyes brimming, slipped quietly away.

The hurt of it all had not lasted beyond two vodka martinis, giving way almost instantly to an anger that burned like fire in the pit of her stomach. It was an anger that Janine knew could be productive, that could be harnessed to subtly augment the situation and tilt the balance back in her favour. It was an anger that she could utilise - an anger that would ultimately achieve results.

Janine's father had taught her the value of strong character and a determined mind: if you are presented with a problem, do not ignore it or hide away - you must fight. Remove or neutralise your inconvenient complication by any means necessary, and then move on. Janine knew her problem was of her own making - she had brought Camille into Arnaud's life and it would be up to her to ensure that she ultimately exited it again. A carefully crafted intervention must be executed, with the end result being revival of a love Janine had nurtured for more years than she could even recall.

In the end, there was no master plan as such - simply an invitation to Camille for a stroll in the cool autumn air. Under pretense of social fatigue, Janine had convinced the unsuspecting adulteress to meet her in an isolated spot far from prying eyes or damning witness. They met close to the cleansing waters of a river Janine had known and trusted since she was a child; she knew the flowing mass would not let her down.

Linking the arm of her victim, Janine had guided Camille past benches and bulrushes, teasing the air with calm and idle chatter as she coaxed the nubile mademoiselle towards her fate. A flick of the wrist and the slim little knife appeared from a hidden pocket in Janine's petticoat; the blade glinted threateningly in the watery afternoon sunlight but escaped Camille's notice until the last second.

The surprise of it all was caught in Camille's expression, mouth hanging open in a perfectly round *oh!* as Janine lunged with conviction and completed her task. Camille gasped and staggered backwards. Eyes fixed on Janine, she swayed slightly, performing a veritable *danse macabre* amid the sun-dappled wildflowers.

A flash of understanding momentarily crossed the fated female's face; Janine's cold and unwavering glare confirmed discovery of the affair and her unwavering intention to reclaim what had been taken. Camille offered a brief yet futile attempt at words before drifting to the ground like a fallen leaf, silent in her final *adieu*.

For a moment, Janine had not been able to not move. She had simply stood, weapon in hand, staring down at the lifeless body of her former friend. It was the chirping that roused her and she had turned to see him sitting there, a few short yards away: *le petit oiseau*. Inquisitive, suspicious, judging. The little bird had watched Janine as she moved quickly towards the dead Camille, as she glanced over her shoulder - left and right and left again - to ensure no human eyes were tracking her dastardly exploits. Janine had dropped to her knees, ready to submerge her problems in the murky depths of the rushing river and still the little bird watched, quiet and keen and calm.

Drawing on every last ounce of strength, Janine had heaved Camille once, twice, a third time, rolling the not-so-dearly departed over and over until she tumbled down the bank and disappeared with a splash. Rising slowly and with tiny beads of sweat forming on her pale forehead, Janine had felt the gaze of her avian spectator burning furiously into her back. She had turned, met his eyes, and felt the cold rush of guilt creep quietly over her pale skin as he continued to observe. Voicing his disapproval with a short and shrill *chirrup*, the bird had lifted himself into the air and disappeared with the breeze, leaving Janine alone on the riverbank with the gravity of what she had done.

In the weeks that followed, thoughts of Camille had been few for Janine. The void of Camille's absence was marked only by an empty chair in the patisserie, and felt briefly on Janine's now solo shopping trips for the latest Louboutin heel. Janine had fabricated a convincing tale of Camille's absconsion, a tale which Arnaud had reluctantly swallowed. Though he had briefly mourned the loss of his extracurricular pursuit, his heart had soon defaulted to its previous romance at the realisation that Camille was not to return. Janine had won her battle and settled victoriously back into a life that she only recently had felt to be slipping away.

If it hadn't been for the little bird, Janine's mind might have been left untroubled by her covert transgressions. Only when she saw him did she falter - and saw him she did. The bird would appear in the unlikeliest of places and at the most inconvenient of times - landing on the boudoir balcony as she and Arnaud shared breakfast; calling to her from a lime tree in Le Jardin de Tuileries as she strolled in the sunshine at lunch; and settling himself at the next table in the courtyard of a Montmartre bistro as she sipped Dom Perignon and slurped down oysters. Logic told Janine that it wasn't the same creature - that a single winged beast would not pursue her so openly around the streets of Paris to remind her of all that she had done. Yet her gut told her otherwise. And when she saw her feathered follower, she recognised him in a heartbeat. The bird was a living reminder of the crime she had committed - of the sin that would endure a thousand hail Mary's - ensuring she would never quite be able to forget the lengths to which she had gone to keep hold of her love.

The bird could never relay the events of that crisp Parisian afternoon, yet his presence in Janine's life grew increasingly intolerable. Soon, Janine couldn't stand to catch even a glimpse of a beak or a wing before losing her composure almost entirely. Friends noted the change in her demeanour, yet Janine brushed away their concerns with the wave of a hand and a casual mention of work worries. Anxiety dug tracks into Arnaud's brow as Janine hissed at the morning birdsong and threw stones at willows full of birdlife in the park, yet no one could have guessed the reason for Janine's progressively volatile behaviour. And no one could have anticipated what was to come next.

As the dawn of a late spring morning broke over the sleepy streets of Saint Germain-des-Prés, Janine awoke once more to the now cruelly familiar chirruping sound of *le petit oiseau*. Arnaud remained deep in slumber as Janine scrambled out of their bed and crept on tiptoe across the room to the little glass door. Through pale silk drapes, she could see him sitting proudly on the wrought iron railings that enclosed their little outside terrace. He chirped again, his gaze fixed on where she stood in the shadows, and quick as a lightning bolt Janine felt all reason leave her. In a split-second she was on the balcony, face to face with her winged tormentor; neither of them moved for one long moment, and then:

A lunge. A shriek. Leaping and grasping, cheeping and gasping, Janine's hands around the neck of the tiny bird and a guttural scream of triumph from the murderous madame as she foresaw the demise of her affliction. But a slip and the dull *thud* of iron on breastbone interrupted her triumph. The air abruptly escaped from her chest and Janine managed a low moan of recognition as she overbalanced. She glimpsed the damp avenue four stories below, deserted in the pre-dawn half-light, and she grasped desperately at the cold iron balustrade, before tumbling awkwardly over the edge.

The police arrived in tandem, sirens savagely cutting the quiet air and reverberating around the 6th arrondissement. Two little squad cars mounted the pavement with men in uniform rushing out towards the spot where Janine laid stock still in the middle of the road. The hem of her nightgown had torn and waved lazily now in the early morning breeze. Unseeing eyes stared quietly up at the sky as a streak of scarlet trickled slowly from nose to ear.

The little bird gazed quizzically at the scene from where he perched on the chimney of a nearby building, the sudden departure of a soul from this earth so far beyond his simple understanding. He sat for a minute more as events on the street beneath him began to unfold. Crowds were beginning to gather as the little bird shifted his weight and shook his wings.

A misty veil of drizzle fuzzed the atmosphere. With a single, short *chirrup* and another shake of his feathers, *le petit oiseau* took off into the hazy pastel morning.

THE LEICESTER WRITES SHORT STORY PRIZE 2019

The Last of the Horse Watchers
MARK NEWMAN

She stares out at fields, this wife of mine; not happy unless she is surrounded by greenery.

'I was a tree in another life,' she says, holding each arm up and bending slightly at the elbow.

If I stare long enough branches sprout and leaves burst open, her face and torso lost in the foliage. Her legs join and all that remains of her are her shoes.

After we married I wanted to live in the city with the roar of traffic and people, or by the ocean with the roar of sea and wind.

'I want to live in the fields,' she said. 'Gather enough trees together, blow a breeze and they too will roar.'

So we moved to this house, in these fields, so far from other people. It had taken so long to find her; I was not prepared to lose her over location. Besides, I was proud to be all the company she wished for.

And I have tried, but I find the silence oppressive, clamping headphones to my ears and turning the music up, drowning out birdsong with drum and bass. The stillness in front of my eyes eats into my brain.

I drive up to the city and squeeze myself between people in busy, noisy bars but my wife will not come.

'I am happy here,' she says.

In each hotel room I slide the chair in front of the window, turn out the lights and watch the city breathe, feeling the warmth of light pollution against my face, pressing my hand to the glass, happy to be part of something.

Alice calls me on the phone.

'Getting your fix?' she says.

'Yep,' I say. 'Fully recharged.'

And by the middle of the night I am pining for her more than I crave the city.

We go out for walks and I am not blind to the beauty. But to me this fertile land is barren because I see nothing man-made, nothing worth walking towards.

She objects out here when I wear bright colours. She wants me in browns and greens so I fade into the background.

'You will turn around one day and I will be gone,' I say, 'And how will you ever find me?'

She looks worried then as if I have given her a warning.

'Can I not wear blue,' I say. 'For the sky?'

She drops her head slightly and looks at me as if over glasses. If there are other people out here they too are in browns and greens and disappear. I long to see a cyclist in fluorescent yellow, cutting across my sightlines.

When we want to rest we stop where we are and lay on the ground, her neck resting on my arm.

The trees rustle their leaves, their whispered conversation seductive, and I almost succumb, can feel my mind clearing, but my own voice calls out inside my head and does not let me slip too far.

When I look at Alice, lying calmly with eyes closed and a serene grin, it is not hard to imagine her brain has shut down; that if I shook her to rouse her I would have a hard time bringing her back. I sit up and grip on to my knees and wait for her to decide where we will go next.

The route we take most cuts through trees, crosses streams, dissects a stone circle and after an hour reaches a field of horses. There are thirty or so and my heart lifts to see them, because here, at last, are other conscious beings. We never see anyone with them, but they are well looked after. They have hay to eat and have covers on their backs when the weather turns. If I come alone then one or two of them trot towards me and I stroke their faces and tell them my feelings, happy to have a chance to talk of the city. When Alice is with me they charge *en masse*, flocking to her, pushing against each other to get close.

'Everyone loves you,' I say.

They are beautiful creatures to me, with eyes full of unbearable sadness.

'It is the knowledge they carry,' she says, and I do not know if she mocks me or if she believes what she says. 'They must trust there are still horse watchers.'

I shake my head, but I love to listen to the things she says. It would be nice to see the world the way she does.

'You're still looking for the way back up the rabbit-hole, aren't you?'

She laughs. 'My mother told me of the horse watchers. Horses are not from this world, you have only to look at them to see the truth of it.'

I can see why folklore persists in remote places. To succumb to the silence is to allow all possibilities in. I can believe a horse is not of this world.

'They have lost their way back,' Alice is saying, 'that is why they look so sad. They are too graceful for this world; they are watching for the person who will lead them home. The Gods gave men this task; they are the horse watchers. They watch the horses and seek their way home. There are few left who remember what they are looking for.'

Alice tells a tale well; when we have a child she will fill its world with wonder. I stare into the eyes of the nearest horse and find myself hoping it finds its way home. In its eyes I can believe they are looking for something and when they find it they will be happy again, joyous even.

In the night, while Alice sleeps, I hope she is watching out for me; that she will see the sadness in my eyes as I yearn for the city. That she will lead me home before I have to ask to go.

When I am inside I try to pretend that the world is whirring on outside these walls, but the endless space bleeds in. While my wife sips wine and flicks through a magazine I am left with thoughts I never had to contemplate before.

How long would it take an ambulance to arrive; if one of us was alone and trapped who could hear us call?

We watch a film about four friends in a house in the middle of nowhere persecuted by a serial killer. It is one I have watched before and enjoyed but midway through I have to feign tiredness and leave the room.

I take an encyclopaedia from the bookcase in the hall, sit on the stairs and watch Alice's silhouette through the frosted glass, casting occasional nervous glances over my shoulder. I find the entry I am looking for. I know nothing of horses, apart from what my wife has told me, and I sit there, while Alice screams at the film and giggles, reciting the parts of the horse over in my head. Pastern, coronet, fetlock. Gaskin, withers, forelock. Would it temper Alice's romantic view of them to read the first sentence of the encyclopaedia entry? 'The horse is an odd-toed ungulate mammal.'

Alice busies herself. She paints, she sews; she likes to be creative. I leave her be and trace the path of our walks alone. In the stone circle I stand dead centre and address the stones as if they were people. I ask them for their histories, and almost hear them reply. Here at least I feel some human connection. These are man-made in the loosest sense - men must have brought these here, lifted them upright. People once gathered here.

I lie on my back at the base of one of them, imagine myself small, staring up at skyscrapers. The clouds roll by above and the motion fools my eye into thinking the stone is falling; that it will drop and crush me.

'What do you think went on at the stone circle?' I say to Alice when I return home. 'Sacrifices and ritual? Sordid dances?'

'Maybe it was just a place to come together and discuss the day,' she says.

'Maybe,' I say. 'It is the gate the horse watchers are seeking.'

She turns to me with a quizzical look, as if she has a question to ask then, but she says nothing and I link my arm with hers.

'The horse watchers must be looking for a pathway back to the Gods,' I say. 'Because, the horse was created by the God Poseidon, in an unsuccessful attempt to woo the Goddess Demeter.'

'I can't imagine being unimpressed by a man who created the horse for me,' Alice says.

'Well, he was the God of the sea and spent most of his day underwater, so maybe the cons outweighed the pros. Plus, she was his sister.'

This house engulfs the sounds around it, whispering and creaking, still communicating with the trees it once stood beside. Do the trees growing alongside now pass its messages on? Do they bend in time, one to the other, sending these missives along?

'The woman,' they say, 'now *she* belongs here. She thinks she can turn the man to her ways, but he will not be changed.'

'But I do not mind,' I whisper then, to whichever part of this house will listen. 'I do not mind at all.'

In the morning she is gone and there is no note to calm my sudden fears.

I stand at the door and call her name, embarrassed to yell into the silence. I dress hurriedly and begin to follow the path of our familiar walk. There is nothing to signify she has walked this way recently, though I do not know what I expect to see. Cutting through the trees is oppressive; they seem closer than usual, their whispers louder, but they tell me nothing. At the stream I catch the glint of fishes as I cross and I almost point them out as I do when Alice is with me. At the stone circle I ask the stones to help me; they sit impassive. I hope for one to fall and point out the direction I should take.

In the field beyond, the horses gallop, round and round, neighing loudly, the sound carrying like laughter. There is no sign of Alice and from here I can see for miles. I sink to the ground and lean against one of the stones. Here I realise that though I had always been running towards Alice, it was not the same for her. She had been stood still as I came to meet her; she had not even been heading my way.

When the sound stops it is sudden and the quiet that descends is cloying. When I turn around the horses are gone. I move frantically, crashing through hedgerows to get into their field. I find her shoes, neatly positioned at the base of a tree, and I lean my head against its trunk and listen to nothing.

The Edge of Love
RICHARD HOOTON

She's with another man. A stranger; to me at least. They're sitting brazenly in the centre of Starbucks on Market Street on a Tuesday afternoon. Her with a latte, all milky soft and white. Him a cappuccino, a dusting of chocolate sprinkled over the murky surface.

I hang around on the other side of the giant window that frames them, caught in two minds. What's worse: to watch or not know? Rachel didn't spot me following her here. She'd just breezed in and lowered herself into a chair at his table, confirming my suspicions after the growing distance between us and those increasing absences.

I make a choice. Creeping in through the open door, I keep out of Rachel's line of vision. Masked by the noise and bustle of the busy coffee shop, I quietly order a double espresso, having a sudden urge for something that will wake me up and keep me alert. A pop ballad is playing; some woman singing about 'the best thing I never had.'

The waitress, wrapped in a black apron bearing streaks of yellow, feigns a smile as she hands me my drink. The saucer shakes in my hand, dark liquid splashing over the cup's brim and stinging my skin. Managing to retain my grip, I take a seat near the counter, positioning myself far enough away from them that Rachel won't notice me but I can still see her. The air is thick, as if the heat and steam from all the brewing have created storm clouds that have become trapped indoors. A sickly sweet smell of roasted coffee beans and cinnamon infiltrates the room.

It's a Tardis of a place, much bigger on the inside than it looks. They're just one couple among many; seemingly innocuous, seemingly innocent. I scan the room. Near the window sits a teenage girl with a laptop, tapping away without a care in the world, a caramel shortbread crumbling onto a small plate next to the machine. Two empty tables away, a student is on his phone, scrolling down the screen, smiling one moment, grimacing the next. Beside him, a family of five occupy two tables shoved together; the young children restless, legs kicking legs – the tables' and each other's – the mother looking harassed, the father ignoring them, but still all together as one. Behind them an old lady sits alone, nursing an empty cup, presumably waiting for a daughter or husband or someone else important in her life.

Then there's Rachel. She's wearing the red pencil dress that shows off her figure. The black leather jacket that she looks so good in is draped around the back of her chair. Scarlet lipstick enhances the fullness of her lips. Bronzer swept beneath sharp cheekbones defines them even more. Thick eyelashes curl upwards. The makeup isn't needed; she's perfect without it.

I look at him. He is of medium build, medium height, medium looks; nothing special. Around her age, so no sugar daddy or frivolous toy boy. He's dressed all in black as if he's stepped straight from my nightmares. The clothes are casual: jeans and t-shirt, the sleeve frayed slightly where his bicep ripples.

I take a sip of coffee but it's too bitter. Tearing the top of a sachet of sugar with a satisfying rip, I pour the contents into my drink, watching them sink to the bottom. Lifting the silver teaspoon, I catch sight of my face in its curvature: large and grotesque, a gurning baboon of a visage. I stir and stir, spoon clinking against porcelain. The mixture bubbles and froths as I contemplate what to do.

Animated in conversation, I don't think they'd notice anyone else here, never mind me. As much as I strain, I can't hear what they're saying over the constant hum of noise: the music, the whirr and clanging of the coffee machine, the rise and fall of chatter, the clanking of cups and cutlery. I can only watch as if it were a piece of silent theatre. They're too close, too cosy. He smiles and Rachel's lips mirror his, a conspiratorial look passing between.

My stomach flips, a cold nausea rising through me. In a perverse way, the sensations remind me of the moment I first saw her three years ago; the most beautiful creature I'd ever seen, her surroundings paling into insignificance.

I'd stumbled to where she stood, poised behind the menswear counter of a department store, and hesitantly handed over the dark green sweater, my fingers shaky in contrast to her gracefulness as she gathered it from me then folded it into the neatest of packages. Her deep blue eyes captivated me as the till roll churned out my receipt. No words passed but she flashed me a knowing smile. My gut lurched as if flying through turbulence. Sweat saturated my palms. I never thought she'd be interested in the likes of me.

Frequent trips followed to purchase clothes I knew would remain in the darkest recesses of my wardrobe. All for a chance to glimpse her. A heady maelstrom of elation and fear when I saw her; unbearable agony when she wasn't there.

A minor disturbance distracts me from my thoughts. A wasp has entered the coffee shop to a yelp from laptop girl. It buzzes around her, enticed by the sweetness of the caramel shortbread. She panics, flaps a flimsy menu at the pest, misses it completely. It's too agile and clever for her efforts, swooping in and out. And too determined, too fixed on its prize, to give up. She's trapped now in a game of survival; either it will sting her or she will eventually swat and kill it. But then it will become a martyr, releasing pheromones to attract other wasps. People watch, grateful that it's not them under attack, while silently judging her reaction.

Rachel and the man don't notice, they have eyes only for each other. He leans towards her, his stubble almost touching her smooth cheek, his lips close to her ear, and whispers something. Something amusing presumably as she flicks back her hair and emits a schoolgirl giggle, her face flushed.

From behind me bursts the mechanical squeal of beans being grinded. I pick up my cup but it's hard to sip coffee when you feel you could vomit at any moment. Another song starts; another power ballad. The singer warbles about 'bleeding love.'

I wonder whether to intervene or leave. Instead, I just stare into the brown liquid. Like a drowning man, our past flashes before my eyes, a history I cling to as if it were a life-raft.

Our relationship developed slowly; it took a while to get Rachel to notice me properly. It was as old-fashioned a courtship as that word implies. Love letters through the post, red roses left on stone doorsteps, cuddly toys delivered to her workplace. Each a little token, a gesture, building into a monument. Every single one worth it in the end as she became the chorus to my verse. I hold onto the memories like a collector cherishes his curiosities.

Movement attracts my attention. Laptop girl has finally struck the wasp with the menu, flinging it from the air onto the table where it staggers. Dazed, it manages to fly to the window, banging itself against the glass in frustration and rage. We all know it will resume its attack as soon as it's recovered.

My eyes turn to Rachel, where they used to find their solace. She seems to be moving closer and closer and closer to him. His hand grazes hers. I almost stand up but control myself, muttering under my breath as I clutch the table leg to keep me anchored. His fingers snake up her palm. Controlling my breathing, I gaze at an abandoned plastic cup on their table, just melting ice cubes left inside.

As I look back, a thickset man in a heavy coat lurches onto a seat in front of me, blocking her out like an eclipse of the sun. Cursing, I attempt to look around his bulk without making it obvious. It's no good, I feel blinded. Near my ear, percolating coffee makes a noise like nails scraping while someone slurps through a straw. It ends with a gurgling. I collect myself before shuffling my chair to the right until I'm able to resume watch. On the woman I see every day. The only woman I've ever loved. The woman whose character is changing before me. I can't believe she's even capable of doing this to me. The loneliest of feelings in the loneliest of moments squirms deep inside. It's then that I realise how lost I'd be without her. My heart beats quicker. It belongs to her, as hers belongs to me.

The waitress hovers at my side, then wipes my table with a damp cloth. I wish she'd go away; it's hard to stay focused with her moving across my eye line.

'You finished?' She nods at my cup. I shake my head, my eyes narrowing. 'You want anything else?'

I put a finger to my lips. She scowls.

'You've been staring at that couple for ages.' Her blonde ponytail shakes, the dark roots pulled back so tight from the scalp that I'm surprised her forehead is able to crease as much as it is. The strip lights above me appear to shine brighter. For a second I glare at her and then soften the look into a smile. She's a slip of a girl, not a woman like Rachel. What can she know about the pain of love?

I retain the smile while waving her away with a flap of my hand. She gives a look as black as mould, then returns behind the counter. I glance around but no-one seems to have taken any notice. The wasp has returned, crawling along laptop girl's shoulder, but she can't see it. Dance music is playing, something about fireworks.

I resume my surveillance just as the man rises to his feet with a scrape of his chair. Now that he's my focus, I think I've seen him before. Was he the guy sniffing around her place before she kept disappearing? Or is he her colleague? He takes a step, bends forward and kisses Rachel on the lips. Snap, snap, snap behind my back is followed by banging, then a rumble and the hiss of steam escaping. I'm in danger of spewing bile across the recently mopped floor that gleams in the intense lights.

The man swaggers towards the toilets. Now's my chance. I decide to confront her but the coward inside restrains me, conscious of an audience. Rachel opens her handbag, takes out a compact mirror and checks her appearance before reapplying her lipstick, following the curves of her lips with a steady hand. All of a sudden, it's clear to me where she's been vanishing to, while I've been waiting for her. My heart feels as if it's tearing in two; it wasn't created to withstand such torment. Pushed too far, I am falling from the edge of love.

Then she looks up. Takes in her surroundings for the first time. Catches my eye.

Her delicate jaw drops, horror spreading across her face. There's no choice now. She looks as startled as a cat suddenly aware it's being watched. Something in her expression causes the sickness inside me to become a lava that threatens to consume everything in its path.

Kicking back my chair, I storm over.

'Who is he?' My voice sounds strangulated.

'Stay away from me.' Hers is tremulous.

I'm so close that I can smell her favourite perfume. It confuses me, makes me want to hold her, kiss her, taste her. Then I remember she's wearing it for him. That magma becomes almost impossible to suppress. I worshipped her. What's left when you've lost your religion?

'Who the hell is he, Rachel?'

She pretends to cower behind the table. 'You know you're not allowed near me.'

I reach out to touch her. She recoils.

Eyes bore into me. I look around. Laptop girl is staring, the wasp tangled in her hair. The family are all facing us, kids gawping. The old lady shakes her head and tuts. The student's eyes have been torn from his mobile. She's humiliating me in front of everyone. It's none of these fuckers' business. Why don't they just fuck off?

I slam my hand on the table and it shudders between us. 'How could you?'

'He won't leave me alone,' she wails. Here we go again. She's so clever. The way she twists the truth, turns the tables on me, makes it look as if *she's* the victim.

'I can't be having this.' The waitress is in my face. She takes a deep breath through trembling lips. 'Please leave.'

I shove her away. Run my hands over my bristling scalp. Her colleagues circle us, swarming from every direction. They steady her. The lights seem to dim until I can no longer see anyone else; there's only Rachel.

'Just tell me who he is.'

Indignation creases her brow. 'Jake's my *fiancé.*'

'What the fuck, Rachel?'

Why does she do this? Why make stuff up? Why play this game? I've never hurt her. Have only ever offered her love. It's as if she gets a kick out of it. Enjoys us carrying on like this. Just won't acknowledge the truth.

I hurl the table to one side. Coffee dregs splatter. Mugs become shards. She screams. Falls from her chair to the floor. I loom over her. Tears spill down her cheeks, smearing black mascara like a painting exposed to rain, spoiling her beauty.

Gasps and gabbling swell to fill my ears with buzzing.

Something grabs my arm.

'Get away from her.'

He's returned. Pulls me back. Steps between us.

I glare at him as if he's an insect that's just stung me.

'Call the police.' He gestures at the waitress. She nods. Flits away.

I can't contain it anymore. It's erupting through me. She is mine and I won't let anyone take her away.

I free the knife from my pocket, the blade iridescent in the harsh light.

At least one of us will die today.

The Bridge
CATHERINE DAY

Christmas Day ten years ago was when I went to the bridge. I walked there barefoot. I think it was because of some story my mother told me about pilgrims climbing Irish mountains without shoes. The walk to the bridge was a pilgrimage; to me and to so many others. By the time I arrived, the soles of my feet had picked up grit and shards of glass, and I was leaving crimson prints on the sidewalk. But I didn't feel any pain.

The place was busy, which I hadn't expected. I thought that every family holed-up in their houses to eat and booze themselves into oblivion like mine used to. I expected an apocalyptic silence and stillness there; but instead, there were at least two-dozen people milling about. Jogging, cycling, pushing strollers, hanging out with their families. There was a festive atmosphere which perturbed me a little. It jarred with the greyness inside my brain. And the presence of so many people made me feel self-conscious… until I realised that everyone was looking straight through me like I was already a ghost. Everyone, except for her.

Out of nowhere, a woman approached me. The woman was early thirties. Looked rich: big hair, long face, fancy clothes. She smiled and her mouth had this bright red lipstick on it. I remember thinking how white and how beautiful her teeth were. Like shiny bright pearls in her mouth. I instinctively smiled back... but with a closed mouth. I've always been ashamed of my teeth. Another wave of shame to join the others, creating a tsunami of mortification inside me. The woman lunged at me and gripped me by the arm. Her long, painted nails dug into my flesh. Her eyes locked onto mine; and it felt like she was turning me inside-out with that look. She knew. I waited for her to start lecturing. Offering the nice but meaningless platitudes that people throw at the suicidal. Stuff they think helps: *but you have so much to live for...think about the people that love you... things are going to get better... have you tried positive thinking/ jogging/ meditation/ getting a cat? Don't be so goddamn selfish!*

I sneered. Tried to shrug her off but her grip was firm. I was ready to tell her to mind her own goddamn business, but then she pointed down. I followed her finger and looked down at a little girl and she looked up at me. She was no more than four years' old. She had an enormous lollipop in her fist, the size of her face. All the colours of the rainbow. I remember seeing those huge lollipops as a kid and pestering my Mom to buy me one, but she never did. My 240lb mom told me it was because gluttony was sinful, but I knew it was because they were five dollars apiece. Lucky kid to have a mother who could afford to buy her pretty things and looked like she should be on one of those women's panel shows on daytime TV.

'Could you watch her for a moment?' the woman asked.

'Sure,' I replied immediately.

Back then, I didn't even like kids, yet I didn't hesitate for a second. The almost imperceptible weirdness of her request caught me off guard. My brain said 'that's weird' and my gut chimed in and said 'yea, that's definitely fuckin' weird' but a stronger voice inside me piped up and said 'don't be a dick. Watch the fuckin' kid'. And that, ladies and gents, is how so many killers and rapists acquire their victims. Because calculating people count on others not wanting to be a dick to get away with their shit. Ted Bundy on crutches asking a girl for help to load his car? She probably sensed some weirdness. Maybe the limp wasn't convincing or something. But she helps anyway cos she doesn't want to be a dick. I'm not saying this lady was a psychopath, or anything like that, but beware of the weirdness. When your gut starts squirming, that's the time to get the fuck outta there. That's what I do now. Since this happened...

So I ignored all the weirdness. The fact that a woman like her was asking a woman like me to watch over her precious kid; and I took the sticky little hand that was reaching up to me. And I also ignored the look in the woman's eyes, the way her bottom lip wasn't quite steady, the vice-like grip she had on my arm. I ignored it all because I didn't want her to think I was a dick. I didn't want that playing on my mind before I took the leap.

'Now Maisie? You stay with the nice lady,' she said, waving her phone, '...I'm going to take a photo of the pretty bridge now.' Her voice had a strange flatness to it. The little girl reached up with her lollipop and offered me some. I shook my head, felt dizzy. I was in a kind of a daze. The kid was cute and all, but I'd been all ready to go, and I had a bad feeling—

Suddenly, Maisie's mom started running. I say she was running but really, it was track-level sprinting. She was tall. Rangy-limbed. She reached the side in no time at all. And then she was up on the bridge, climbing. Her winter coat flapped behind her in the breeze for a moment, like a superhero cape, and then she went over. She was gone.

Someone screamed: 'a jumper!'

And then there was a lot of screaming. I know some of the screaming belonged to her, but I didn't want to hear any of it. I remembered my phone and my headphones. I turned to Maisie and got down on my haunches so our eyes were level. I asked her if she wanted to listen to some music with me and she nodded. So I popped one of my earphones into her ear, found a YouTube video of some kid's song and pressed 'play'. I closed my other ear over with the palm of my hand, and she followed suit. We both turned and faced away from the bridge, because I didn't want to see anything. But my ears? They still kept tuning into what was happening around us. I kept overhearing things. I heard that Maisie's mother didn't die on impact, like the vast majority of jumpers. Like I had expected to.

'She probably broke every bone in her body—a fall from 25 stories will do that to you,' someone said. And I heard people calling emergency services, people calling other people assholes for filming, people sobbing, people shrieking. There were angry people too. People saying that she had traumatised their kids… ruined their Christmas. And though I felt bad for the woman; I also felt angry, but for different reasons to everyone else.

That woman had been gripping my arm, pointing at the kid, waving her phone… and all the while she was slipping off her Louboutin's and getting ready to run. Sleight of hand like a goddamn magician, or a pickpocket And suddenly it hit me why she picked me. Of course she picked me! It was because she knew! I knew she knew when she grabbed me. She also knew that if I went first she couldn't go. She stole my place. Just like if I'd gone first, I would have stolen hers.

She had royally fucked my plans. She had fucked them in multiple ways. Like she had gone through the entire Karma Sutra of plan-fucking. Because how could I jump now? My courage was gone. My timing was off. My self-talk was drowned-out. And now I couldn't go anywhere because I had this little kid clinging onto my hand, and I couldn't just leave her there alone. I couldn't just leave her there alone. Leave her like her mother had.

But the worst thing of all? The thing that I couldn't get past. The thing I'd never get past… was that she had changed her mind. In that split second, when the cold, hard, hungry current made contact with her body, she changed her mind. I heard her changing her mind; and I'd never forget it.

The hysteria was dying down to a low sob. I needed to offload this kid; so I removed the earbud from her ear.

'What's your name?' I asked her.

'Maisie Jane Jones,' she lisped, before licking the lollipop thoughtfully.

'Where do you live Maisie Jane Jones?' I asked, forcing cheeriness into my voice.

'In my house,' she said, smiling proudly, because she knew that was the right answer.

'And where's your house?'

She peered around, as though hoping to catch sight of it, and shrugged her shoulders.

'Can you describe the street?'

'Umm…' she said. 'It's beside Mr McWuffins house… do you know him? He has yellow hair like Mommy and he's a really good boy.'

I closed my eyes and pinched the bridge of my nose.

'Are you the nice woman?' she asked.

'Probably not.'

'Mommy told me to show the nice woman this after she went away.'

She pulled up her sleeve. There was a phone number scrawled along her arm. I ripped the earbuds from my phone and called it. The man on the other end picked up immediately. There was panic in the voice. Expectation. He expected what was coming. I told him in veiled language and in a soft tone of voice what had happened to his wife. Maisie didn't react to anything I was saying. When she finished with that lollipop she probably began to wonder where her mother might be, but in that moment life was a bright, colourful, sweet-tasting thing. Giving her little hits of sugar. And I began to realise that I needed my own hits of sugar, but I had to stay with Maisie. It would take an hour for him to reach the bridge. I was to spend that hour shooting the breeze with Maisie, my sticky-fisted little anchor. When the man arrived I handed Maisie over to him. He nodded thanks at me, before rubbing his face. His eyes were bloodshot, flitting around. Confused.

'Goodbye, nice lady,' Maisie said as her father led her away. I noticed the abandoned Louboutin's, toppled over where their owner had left them. I slid my feet into them. 'It's the least she owes me', I thought to myself; starting to feel conscious of my appearance. I called an Uber and went home. They reported it on the news a few hours later. They'd pulled a woman's broken body up from the river.

It's ten years to the day since my pilgrimage I still don't have anyone to spend Christmas Day with, though the local feral cat that might take pity on me and pay a visit. I'll look Maisie Jane Jones up on Facebook. I don't know how much Maisie remembers of that day. How much she wants to remember. So I won't message her to ask her how she's doing. Instead, I'll look at photos of her and her father on vacation or sailing or eating ice-cream. I'll tell myself they are all doing fine, because they are smiling. Even though it's obligatory to smile for photos.

The anger towards Maisie's mom is long gone. It's replaced with something else. *I am here because she is not and she'd be here if I was not.* A girl is without her mother on Christmas Day because I didn't drive to the bridge. Because I didn't tell her that her teeth were pretty and her kid was cute. Because I didn't listen to my gut. Because I didn't read her the way she read me. Survivor's guilt is a funny thing.

The want to die is gone too. Something happened that made me glad to be here. It was something ordinary, but it was significant even in its smallness and its mundanity. Perhaps, because of its smallness and mundanity. And after the thing that made me glad to be here happened, I went to the doctor and I asked for help and I was one of the lucky ones, because the help he offered me worked. My days are simple. I feed the feral cat. I go to work. I take my meds and I got to support group meetings. Some days I drink, though I know I shouldn't, but we all need our little hits of sugar.

I take it one day at a time. One day at a time isn't hard. After all, the bridge is always there.

THE LEICESTER WRITES SHORT STORY PRIZE 2019

Afterimage
GRACE HADDON

I walk through Haymarket Bus Station and everyone is dead.

My rucksack bites into my shoulder as I step over a tree root. Ivy drips from the ceiling, trickles down the yellow walls and twists around the timetable billboards. The sun heats up the building like a greenhouse; condensation gathers on the plastic signs. A squirrel sits on top of the departures board, flicking its tail.

I walk. Corpses slump on the metal benches, draped in dead leaves. Twenty years waiting for a bus? Someone should complain.

A few buses are here, rusting in their bays. There's a driver shrivelling under his newspaper, ignoring the commuters waiting for him to open the doors.

The squirrel turns to watch me as I pass beneath it. I show it my middle finger.

I leave the bus station and turn right into Haymarket Shopping Centre. The shade slides over my skin like cloth. Two floors of shops surround me in a ring, their signs faded and smeared with lichen. A sun-whitened banner hangs limp from the balcony: *Visit Boots today for your free Iris consultation and we'll solve any tech problems at 20% off! Do you have #2020vision?*

There are bodies here too, but most are scattered bones. Humanity died out but we left our dogs behind. I sit down on the frozen escalator and swallow a sip of water. My flask is too light, just like my head. Leicester's a nightmare to get to on foot, especially when you can't remember the way. I haven't been here since the Corruption.

Pain spikes through my head and I retch. Need to find supplies. Iris could make this so much easier… but Kimmie would have told me that was stupid.

I stand up slowly, breathing oven-door air. I keep going for her.

In another lifetime, when I was doing my photography degree, I looked at old photos of Leicester. The clock tower was always there: surrounded by horse-drawn carts, then tram tracks, then busy shoppers meeting up for lunch. A stone lodged in time's river, the one constant in a changing world. Today it's an ivy-shrouded sentinel over a dead city. Tinsel trails from it like the legs of a giant spider.

The ground is thick with bodies: husks on the benches, mounds of grass and flowers by glassless shop windows. I pause by the bench. It's still there, inscribed in the plastic: *Astrid!!!* I carved it with a biro the day I finished college. Like I realised my life was tiny, so I left a tiny mark behind. I'm forty now. Doesn't feel like I've changed since then; maybe I had to stay the same when everything changed around me.

Heat ripples up from the bricks. I don't know where I'm going. It's like seeing a familiar place at night and everything's different, except that it's twenty years on and everyone's dead. I have to risk it. If I don't find supplies soon I'll be just another dried-up body like everyone else.

I stand in the doorway of GAME so I don't have to squint. Then I blink three times and force the words from my parched throat. 'Open Iris.'

Nothing happens. I breathe out and lean against the wall. Then words appear in front of me.

Welcome back! Rebooting Iris…

A grid slides across my vision, lines and numbers flashing too fast to see. Everything flickers. Then my Iris is working again.

Failed to obtain wi-fi signal.
Using last known location…
Obtaining cached data…

GALLOWTREE GATE, LEICESTER
Shops near you:
GAME – CLOSED
Boots – CLOSED
Clarks – CLOSED
Highcross Shopping Centre – CLOSED

I blink the text away. 'Need food,' I rasp. 'Find nearest supermarkets.' But my Iris doesn't respond. Maybe the circuitry's gone bad, rotting inside my brain. I get more headaches than I used to.

I step outside and nearly have a heart attack. A bald guy with glasses is smiling at me. Well, not a guy. Just his head. It's floating at eye-level, under the words *STEWART*

KEEL. More heads are nearby: a Chinese woman, a grumpy old lady, a guy with a spider tattoo on his cheek.

Pain lances through my head again. I press my thumbs into my temples and force my eyes to stay open. Each image hovers over a body, or the remains of one. All these years and their Irises still work, responding to mine.

STEWART beams at my outstretched hand. He flickers as I get closer. When I try to touch him, he disappears.

I walk down Gallowtree Gate, and hundreds of dead faces watch me pass. I'm used to death, but only because I convinced myself they weren't people anymore. I look down at the bodies instead, until my neck hurts.

A few people survived the Corruption, mostly the very young and the very old, but many didn't live long. I haven't seen anyone in years. Maybe some of the kids made it to adulthood, had their own kids even. Or maybe they decided to finish what the apocalypse started.

It's like insects crawl on my eyes, pointing at things: *CARD FACTORY, WHSMITH, THE WORKS*. Occasionally it all flickers. The heads move with mine, turning to face me and bobbing with my steps.

I realise I've walked too far when I spot an older, grander building: *NATWEST*. A filthy Labrador whimpers at me from the doorway and retreats into the dark.

Red words appear across my vision. *Program update available. Would you like to update your Iris?*

Despite the heat, suddenly I'm cold. 'Fuck, no.' I blink three times and my vision goes quiet. I retrace my steps and find my own way to Marks and Spencer's. It's back near the clock tower. Easy to miss as it's covered in ivy.

Inside, the ceiling has caved in. Rusting fridges lie under ancient rubble. I scrabble in the dirt for a tin, anything, throwing aside something that feels too brittle to be a tree branch. I'll take even hot dog water right now.

I slice my hand on glass and blood spatters my trainers. I'm so damn thirsty and everyone's dead and Kimmie isn't here. It would be so *easy* to just say yes.

I tilt my hand and watch the blood trickle down my wrist. An accident. Simple human error. The news was always full of fear: someone would bomb us, or swine flu would wipe us out, or global warming would drown us. And the thing that killed us in the end? An accident. Our accident.

I flick my finger, speckling the floor. One little glitch in a string of code. An Iris update file that automatically downloaded to everyone at once. It severed a connection in their brains. Humans evolved almost by accident. Seems almost poetic that an accident should finish us off.

I grab my flask. I drink it all. And when I'm strong enough to walk outside, I leave my rucksack behind.

'Open Iris.'

Iris doesn't have much memory space, but it still has the last video I recorded. My internet was off that day as it interfered with my view of the camera.

It takes nearly ten minutes to get it to play in full screen, since it means obscuring my vision. By the time I've finished disabling the safety protocols, sweat is pouring down my back.

I blink, and it's Christmas. The streets are brick and chewing gum, and bundles of cold people march past me. I spot a blue and white football scarf: did Leicester win again? The clock tower is lit from below, like a kid with a torch about to tell a ghost story. Silver tinsel glitters in a breeze I don't feel.

The world blurs as my eyes water. I walk among the dead and feel twenty again. I'm at university. I eat baked beans and text Kimmie about my latest breakup and do coursework at two in the morning...

But this world is silent. The busker outside Highcross shopping centre flexes his accordion. The sun still rakes my skin and stings my throat. I look and look and drink in the white and blue and silver, not yet a world snatched away.

Phantom hands hover in front of my face: chipping nail varnish, red and green. The camera hovers, moving closer to my eye. I take photos of the clock tower whilst I wait.

I don't feel the hand that taps me on the shoulder. But I see her, all dyed blonde hair and reindeer hairband, grinning and shivering. She mouths a greeting. And she falls.

They all go at once, eyes rolling back in their heads like dolls. Families, students, elderly. Carrier bags regurgitate their contents, cars crash into each other, receipts fly away in the wind. In ten seconds, the world ends. The camera falls from my hands and breaks on the ground.

I trip over something that isn't there and my face smacks into hot brick. The world flickers and leaves behind its broken afterimage.

When I open my eyes the video is gone, but she's still there. She's almost dust from being out here so long, but she's still wearing those stupid reindeer ears. I reach for her and the bones are hot. Above her flickers, barely readable, KIMMIE GREEN. I close my eyes and rest my cheek on the ground. I don't move for a while.

The message appears behind my eyelids, like it's carved into my brain.

Would you like to update Iris?

I lie there, pretending to be just another mound of dirt and ivy. *Do you give up?* is what it should say. *Have you had enough? Do you want to get it over with?*

Yes, I tell it. And the update wheel turns.

I told myself I'd returned to Leicester to find supplies, search for fellow survivors, whatever. But of course that wasn't the real reason.

I've been alone for a long time. It's not like the movies, where a few individuals can rebuild civilisation and save the world. In the Grand Age of Tech Doing Everything For Us, who the hell knows how to survive in the wilderness? Everyone just gave up in the end. I only kept going because I stayed away from Leicester. That way I could pretend everyone was safe. That my old life was here, waiting until I came back for it, and that my sister was still alive.

I look up and the dead faces smile down at me. I stare down Humberstone Gate, where the fairground rides are rusting away. I had my first kiss under this clock tower, on a drunk New Year's Eve. That moment felt so important, once.

Pausing systems… commencing update…

It's like nature has leached all the colour away. Everything is green and brown, even the bodies.

Except for something pink, shimmering in the heat haze. I rub my eyes.

A corpse lies outside Clarks, curled up with one arm outstretched. In its hand is a bunch of wild flowers.

I raise my head. Tiny petals, the colour of raspberries, bloom on fragile hairy stems. It's a defiant little *screw you* amidst the dirt and rot, and it almost makes me smile.

Then I see that the stems have been cut and I realise that they didn't grow there, they were placed. Someone else has been here. And I've just missed my chance.

Failed to obtain Wi-Fi signal. Update unsuccessful.

My breath leaves me in a sob. My heart beats a rhythm against the bricks whilst the sun burns the back of my neck. I'm still here.

And so is Kimmie. I look back at her. Seeing her again was the only thing I ever wanted, but now I don't know what I want anymore. I'm not sure I want to die here.

A name appears above the body holding the flowers. *JASPER MOORE*, a teenager with a shy smile and freckles.

He's special to someone, just like Kimmie. Whoever left the flowers… we have something in common.

I sit up slowly, feeling giddy with the heat. When I came here, I hadn't planned to leave again. But what if there's someone here who needs me? If they're still fighting, maybe I can too. Maybe I'm not finished with this broken world just yet.

Iris flickers. *Would you like to try again?*

Among the dead, I stand up.

THE LEICESTER WRITES SHORT STORY PRIZE 2019

Black Eyes and Love Hearts
VANESSA L. FARMERY

'FIGHT!!'

The word burst out of the boy's mouth before his head had been thrust through the doorway. One look at his face told Mr Grosvenor, generally known as G'vnor by staff and students alike, that this was not just a scuffle over a game of conkers, and he hurriedly put down the equipment he had been setting out for his afternoon session with 4B to dash after young Hildyard.

Outside, a large group of pupils had gathered in the furthest corner of the yard from the buildings and were chanting, 'Fight, fight, fight.' G'vnor could see the two female lunchtime supervisors ineffectively trying to push their way through the crowd. As Mrs Fox was approaching retirement and weighed at least seventeen stone she was not particularly fit, while her assistant was a much younger woman in her first term on the job who lacked confidence. G'vnor pulled out the old Police whistle which he always carried in his pocket and blew it three times.

The chanting stopped and the throng of onlookers parted, as the Red Sea had for Moses, to allow Mr Grosvenor to stride through the gap to the centre where he found the perpetrators still slugging it out. It was a bloody battle, and not a fair one. The significantly smaller of the two boys involved had red streaks down his ripped school shirt but, in spite of this, was still attempting to pummel the parts of his opponent that he could reach.

G'vnor knew the pair of course; as the only Science Master in the school he taught each class and therefore every pupil once a week. The smaller boy, Kevin Jackson, was a gobby little sod and G'vnor was sure, even before the inquisition that was bound to follow, that he would have provoked the physical reaction from Nate Smith.

Not that it would have taken much; Smith was apt to thump first and ask questions not at all. As a regular returning student to the school - some said a recurring nightmare - Smith mostly lived life on the road with his extended family of Irish travellers. The men were horse dealers, scrap merchants and bare knuckle fighters. The women stayed at home in immaculately kept caravans and gained more knowledge of the world from the distorted morality of daytime TV than from society at large. G'vnor liked Nate, in whom he had spotted an untrained intelligence and spark of interest, but he knew that the boy was unlikely ever to take advantage of the opportunities state education purported to offer to all. The lad struggled to read and write, although there was nothing wrong with his general reasoning and ability to analyse results and form conclusions as long as he was allowed to do it verbally. G'vnor had also been impressed by his deftness when handling the equipment they used in practical sessions, the care he took to assemble and place the Bunsen burners, flasks and pipettes, his precise measurement of potions and powders. His results were always spot on.

Kevin, on the other hand, was a boy he just couldn't take to. No more privileged than Nate, Kevin came from what the press called a broken home; his father had gone by the time he was two and his mother had replaced him with a series of disinterested boyfriends who all left her eventually. Kevin had several younger half-brothers and sisters with whom he scrambled for space in their three bed-roomed home which was decorated with the once lurid but now faded sixties wallpaper of the previous tenant. His mother had unsuccessfully tried to paint over it but the house still looked like somebody else's. Kevin was a classic under-achiever; lazy, cocky, irritating, a distraction in the classroom and a minimalist on paper. He wouldn't write a sentence when a word would do, he didn't bother with the formalities of setting out a page with date, title and subtitles, never labelled his scruffy diagrams and did not possess a ruler. 'Just get by,' was his motto in life, and it annoyed the hell out of G'vnor who hated time-wasters - whether that meant someone who wasted their own time or that of other people. Whenever he saw Kevin Jackson he felt like giving him a slap to wake him up, so there was a nasty little bubble of satisfaction that rose to the surface of his conscience briefly when he saw the boy's scarlet spattered face.

Nate was tall and well-built - there were suspicions that he was a year or two older than his parents had said - while whey-faced Kevin was scrawny. That Nate could take Kevin in a scrap was not in doubt, and G'vnor knew that the bigger boy could have inflicted some serious damage if he'd lost control, so he lost no time in pushing between the adversaries and spreading out his arms to separate them. His twenty years as a copper still came in handy from time to time, not least because he had a strong physical presence and exuded an air of authority.

The mob that had surrounded the boys began to melt away as the older woman dispersed them with a sharp, 'Show's over,' and G'vnor kept the boys apart. Kevin was enraged and was shouting about the state of his shirt.

'Take him away, please, Mrs F,' said G'vnor firmly, all the while keeping his hand spread out flat on Nate's chest.

'Now then, lad, calm down,' he advised. He could feel Nate's pounding heart and his barely checked physical strength. The stench of teenage testosterone was thick and unpleasant. Nate's rage got the better of him and he threw a punch. G'vnor knew that such an action would trigger a much more serious set of consequences, but fortunately his old crowd control instincts had kicked in and, as he had a slightly longer reach than the boy, Nate's fist impacted against nothing and floundered impotently in the space between them.

'Inside,' said G'vnor, and in a swift move that he had not performed for a number of years he placed himself behind Nate, gripping the collars of his shirt and jacket. Arm outstretched he steered Nate across the playground and to the doors that led into the school building, the boy still in combat with an imaginary enemy and his arms wind-milling in his attempt to hit someone, or anyone.

The corridor within was long, with several doors off it and, as they marched to the end and the Headmaster's office, Mr Grosvenor could see his various colleagues looking up to see what was going on, craning their necks, raising their eyebrows, rolling their eyes. To most of them, Nate was just a nuisance, here one week and gone the next; sullen, unskilled and anti-social.

G'vnor pushed Nate down solidly onto a chair and sat next to him.

'What's it all about, then, lad?' he enquired.

Nate did not reply, but balled his hands so tightly that his knuckles whitened.

'It would be better for you if you could explain what triggered it, you know.'

Nate muttered something inaudible.

'Speak up! I'm getting on and I'm a bit deaf on that side.'

There was another indistinct pronouncement.

'Alright, take your time, have a think. But something must have sparked that - you've given him a bit of a pasting you know,' G'vnor looked at Nate whose eyes were lowered and whose shoulders were taught. 'Just tell the Head what happened; he'll listen. But if you say nothing, he's nothing to listen to, has he?'

Nate shrugged and his head hung lower.

The matter was dealt with. It took the best part of the afternoon but the Head - who was not a man without empathy - got to the bottom of things. As G'vnor had thought, Kevin had made a series of inflammatory remarks and goaded Nate into hitting out first. The impact, which had caused his nose to bleed, also gave him a black eye which Kevin wore with a swaggering pride until it faded from a purplish-grey to a less impressive jaundiced yellow. Both boys were suspended for the rest of the week and their parents sent for.

When they came back to school on the following Monday, Kevin was as cocky as ever but Nate was more subdued and had a black eye of his own. 'Rough justice,' said the Head, grimly, and did not inquire too deeply as to its origin.

The lunchtime saw Mr Grosvenor in his classroom-cum-laboratory as usual, this time seated at the heavy old workbench which bore the stains and scars of two decades of science experiments. He was marking the efforts of 2A to design an experiment to test the strength of plastic bags and it was like wading through treacle.

Suddenly, the door opened and Nate Smith walked through it decisively. G'vnor sat up straight and looked him in the eye, noting the bruise at the top of his cheek, and hoped he wasn't in the mood for retribution.

The boy advanced towards the workbench at an unfaltering pace and stopped a foot short of touching it. His hand slipped into his pocket and he pulled out a crumpled white paper sweet packet and untwisted one side of it. He peered in and, with fingers that were none too clean, extracted a single sweet which he placed carefully in front of Mr Grosvenor. The teacher looked down and saw, to his surprise, that the sweet was a love-heart, one of those pastel-coloured confections favoured by the girls for the sentimental messages printed on them in a garish vermillion hue. He looked at Nate and then back at the sweet.

'*YOU ARE MY CHUM*,' it boldly declared.

'Well, thank you, Nate,' he said, picking it up.

'Sir,' said Nate.

Mr Grosvenor held out his right hand. Ned looked at it in bewilderment for a moment before realising what he must do. His face split into a broad, seldom seen grin which revealed a glint of gold behind a canine and he swiftly spat on his own right hand and slapped it into the outstretched one, shaking it twice with a vice-like grip. Then he turned and took his leave; of the classroom, of the school, of the system.

Mr Grosvenor had just witnessed Nate Smith coming of age.

THE LEICESTER WRITES SHORT STORY PRIZE 2019

About the Authors

Cath Barton is an English writer who lives in South Wales. She won the New Welsh Writing AmeriCymru Prize for the Novella 2017 for *The Plankton Collector*, now published by New Welsh Review under their Rarebyte imprint. Cath's collection of short stories, *The Garden of Earthly Delights*, inspired by the work of the sixteenth-century Flemish artist Hieronymus Bosch, and including the story *California Dreamin'*, will be published by Retreat West Books in early 2021. The collection was completed with the assistance of the Literature Wales Mentoring Scheme, supported by the National Lottery through the Arts Council of Wales.

Dianne Bown-Wilson was born in England, grew up in New Zealand and now lives in Dartmoor National Park. Her stories have either won prizes or been placed in competitions including the Fish Prize, Exeter Writers, Henshaw Prize, The Momaya Annual Review, Writing Magazine, Writers Forum, and the Bedford Writing Competition. A collection of thirty-two of her successful stories, Instructions for Living and Other Stories was published in 2016. Her story Get Along Without You Now was Highly Commended in the 2018 Leicester Writes Short Story competition.

Sharon Boyle has always been a writer in her head, making things up about her life to make it more interesting than it could ever hope to be. She penned a few words, and, after having the nerve to send off half-baked, excruciating efforts, eventually started to see her short stories and flash pieces being published on-line and in print. She has won the *HISSAC* and *Exeter Writers* short story comps.

Dan Brotzel won the 2018 *Riptide Journal* short story competition, and was highly commended in the Manchester Writing School competition 2018. He has words in places like *Ellipsis, Reflex Fiction, Cabinet of Heed, Bending Genres, The Esthetic Apostle, Spelk, Ginger Collect, The Pithead Chapel* and *Fiction Pool*. His first collection of short stories, *Hotel du Jack*, will be published early 2020. He is also co-author of a comic novel, *Kitten on a Fatberg* (Unbound).

Donna Brown lives in Cheshire. She writes short stories and flash fiction, and is currently working on a novel. Donna's flash fiction has been published on *The Casket of Fictional Delights* website, and she won the Winchester Writers' Festival Short Story Prize in 2018.

Mary Byrne lives in Loughborough. She is an artist as well as a writer, and worked as an adult art tutor until recently. She describes her writing as visually aware and her art as narrative-based. Mary has had several stories published in literary magazines, most recently in *The Coffee House*, and is at present working on a historical novel. She is from Scotland originally but has lived all over Britain, from Aberdeen to London, working in places as varied as a Blackpool Rock factory and the Map Department of the National Archives.

Selma Carvalho is the author of three non-fiction books documenting the Goan presence in colonial East Africa. She led the Oral Histories of British-Goans Project archived at the British Library Kings Cross. Her fiction has been published by *Litro* and *Lighthouse* among others and appears in 12 anthologies. She has received a nod from numerous short story competitions, including Fish and Bath, notably as a shortlist finalist for the London Short Story Prize and winner of the Leicester Writes Prize 2018. Her collection of short stories was longlisted for the prestigious SI Leeds Literary Prize 2018.

Catherine Day Prior to qualifying as a solicitor, Catherine received a bachelor's degree in English and French Literature and a master's degree in French Autobiography from University College Dublin. She started writing seriously in 2016, and completed it in 2017. She is currently working on her second novel and a collection of short stories while looking for a literary agent. Her short story 'A Stalked Animal' was recently published in the online journal, *Delay Fiction* and she was shortlisted for the 2019 Retreat

West First Chapter Competition with her first novel *The Darkest Harbour*.

Vanessa L. Farmery was born in East Central Africa, under a wandering star which she has been following ever since. A self-confessed global nomad, she has travelled extensively although she calls the East Riding of Yorkshire home. She has mainly worked in education but has also been employed in the retail and care industries and in administration. Vanessa regards all experience as fair game and often writes about situations, people and places she has encountered throughout her life. Although she considers herself mainly as a writer of fiction there are often elements of biography and creative non-fiction in her stories.

Cindy George has been a radio advertising copywriter, music journalist, writer of romances for teen magazines, and farmhand on a banana plantation, and is now an author, journalist, copywriter and poet living in Coventry. Her work has been published by The Fiction Desk, Arachne Press, and Here Comes Everyone among others. She has an MA in Writing from the University of Warwick, and is now working on her first novel.

Bev Haddon lives in Oadby with her husband and two daughters. She retired a few years ago, and now moonlights as a mystery shopper and product tester, with occasional stints as a lab rat for University of Leicester. She has been published by Write In For Charity and was shortlisted for the Leicester Writes 2017 competition. She loves toast, Horlicks and walks along the seashore. Her hobbies are collecting Project Club Books (remember them?) and running a Doctor Who fan site. Waitrose is her safe word.

Grace Haddon is a Leicester writer of fantasy fiction. She holds a BA in Creative and Professional Writing from the University of Nottingham, where she edited the class anthology *Vices and Virtues*. She is on the writing team of Write in For Charity, a Leicester charity initiative which produces e-books. In 2015 she won Malorie Blackman's Project Remix competition, and she was on the judging panel of the Leicester Writes Short Story Competition in 2017. Her story *Afterimage* was inspired by old photos of Leicester's clock tower, and seeing how the city slowly changed over time.

Debz Hobbs-Wyatt lives and works in Essex as a full-time writer and editor. She has had over thirty short stories published and won the inaugural Bath Short Story Prize in 2013. She has also been nominated the US Pushcart prize and shortlisted in the Commonwealth Short Story Prize. Her debut novel *While No One Was Watching* was published by Parthian Books and she has several other novels in various stages of development. She edits professionally and mentors aspiring writers.

Sara Hodgkinson is a native northern Brit with a penchant for good food, well-thumbed books and long walks in the calming countryside. Sara has spent much of the last decade travelling the world, meeting great people and absorbing a kaleidoscope of cultures. She has lived in Singapore and Australia, and is currently back in the UK working as a freelance content writer from her home in the hills of Lancashire. In her spare time, she conjures fiction with the help of her two eccentric cats, red wine and a steady supply of decaffeinated tea.

Born and brought up in Mansfield, Nottinghamshire, **Richard Hooton** studied English Literature at the University of Wolverhampton before becoming a journalist and communications officer. He has worked as a reporter and news editor for several regional newspapers. Turning his hand to creative writing in his spare time, Richard has been longlisted and shortlisted in numerous competitions, including winning contests run by Segora, Artificium Magazine, Audio Arcadia and Henshaw Press and being placed in others. He lives in Mossley, near Manchester.

Emma Lee's short stories have been published in anthologies and magazines including Fairlight Books, 'Gentle Footprints' (Bridgehouse Publishing) and 'Extended Play' (Elastic Press). She was runner-up in Writing Magazine's Annual Ghost Story Competition. Her most recent poetry collection is *Ghosts in the Desert* (IDP,

2015), *The Significance of a Dress* is forthcoming from Arachne in 2020. She is Reviews Editor at The Blue Nib, co-edited *Over Land, Over Sea: poems for those seeking refuge* (Five Leaves, 2015).

Thomas Morgan is a writer from Worthing in West Sussex. He graduated from The University of Sussex with a degree in Film Studies. Thomas started writing short fiction at the beginning of the year. This is his first published piece.

Mark Newman has been shortlisted for the Costa Short Story Award, highly commended in the New Writer Prose & Poetry Awards and Bristol Prize longlisted. His work has won competitions judged by Alison Moore, Tania Hershman and David Gaffney. He has been published in Fireworks Quarterly, Fiction Desk and Paper Swans. He has eight stories in the Retreat West competition anthology Inside These Tangles, Beauty Lies and his debut short story collection My Fence is Electric & Other Stories will be published by Odyssey Books in February 2020.

Patricia M Osborne was born in Liverpool and spent time in Bolton as a child. She now lives in West Sussex. Patricia is a novelist, poet, and short story writer. Her poetry and short stories have been published in various literary magazines and anthologies, and her debut novel, House of Grace, was published in March 2017. Patricia has an MA in Creative Writing with University of Brighton. She gains inspiration from visiting local lakes, parks, and National Trust Properties. Hobbies include walking, playing the piano, socialising, reading, photography, and painting with watercolours.

Judging Panel

Susmita Bhattacharya was born in Mumbai. Her short fiction has been widely published, been nominated for the Pushcart Prize and broadcast on BBC Radio 4. Her novel, *The Normal State of Mind*, was published in 2015 by Parthian (UK) and Bee Books (India). It was long listed for the Words to Screen Prize by the Mumbai Association of Moving Images (MAMI). She teaches contemporary fiction at Winchester University and also facilitates the Mayflower Young Writers workshops, a SO:Write project based in Southampton.

Rebecca Burns is a writer of short stories and fiction. Her work has been published in over thirty online and print journals. She has won or been placed in many competitions including the Fowey Festival of Words and Music Short Story Competition. Her debut collection of short stories, *Catching the Barrmundi*, was published by Odyssey Books in 2012 and was longlisted for the Edge Hill Award. Her second collection, *The Settling Earth* (2014) was also longlisted for the Edge Hill. Her debut novel, *The Bishop's Girl*, was published in 2016, and her third collection of short stories, *Artefacts and Other Stories*, appeared in 2017, both again published by Odyssey Books. Her second novel, *Beyond the Bay* was published in September 2018.

Jonathan Taylor is an author, editor, lecturer and critic. His books include the poetry collection, *Cassandra Complex* (Shoestring, 2018), the novel *Melissa* (Salt, 2015), the short story collection, *Kontakte and Other Stories* (Roman, 2013), and the memoir *Take Me Home* (Granta, 2007). He is editor of the anthology *High Spirits: A Round of Drinking Stories* (Valley, 2018). He directs the MA in Creative Writing at the University of Leicester. He lives in Leicestershire with his wife, the poet Maria Taylor, and their twin daughters, Miranda and Rosalind.